# ARMS RACE

Nic Low is an author and artist of Ngai Tahu Maori and European descent. Born in Christchurch, he now divides his time between Melbourne and a bush retreat near Castlemaine. Nic's fiction, essays and criticism have appeared in the *Big Issue*, *Monthly*, *Griffith Review*, *Lifted Brow*, *Art Monthly* and *Australian Book Review*. He was runner-up in the 2013 Overland Short Story Prize, shortlisted for the 2012 Commonwealth Short Story Prize and won the 2011 GREW Prize for Non-fiction. Until recently he ran Asialink's international writing program. He is working on his next book, a literary exploration of New Zealand's Southern Alps. dislocated.org

# ARMS RACE

## AND OTHER STORIES

## NIC LOW

TEXT PUBLISHING
MELBOURNE AUSTRALIA

The Text Publishing Company
Swann House
22 William Street
Melbourne Victoria 3000
Australia
textpublishing.com.au

Early versions of some of these stories were published in *Griffith Review*
('Octopus'), *Overland* ('Rush') and the *Big Issue* ('Slick').

First published in 2014 by The Text Publishing Company

Cover & page design by W.H. Chong
Typeset in Garamond Premier Pro by J & M Typesetting
Printed in Australia by Griffin Press

National Library of Australia Cataloguing-in-Publication entry:
Author: Low, Nic
Title: Arms race : and other stories / by Nic Low
ISBN: 9781922147981 (paperback)
ISBN: 9781922148988 (ebook)
Dewey Number: A823.4

This book is printed on paper certified against the Forest Stewardship
Council® Standards. Griffin Press holds FSC chain-of-custody
certification SGS-COC-005088. FSC promotes environmentally
responsible, socially beneficial and economically viable management
of the world's forests.

This project has been assisted by the Commonwealth Government
through the Australia Council, its arts funding and advisory body.

# CONTENTS

*For Beth*

*For Hikatea and Geoff*

# OCTOPUS

AT TEN the sun finally sets and the pub fills up and the news comes on. It's my round. A couple of aunties up the back give me a nod but everyone else seems *pakeha*. The bloke behind the bar looks down at my tarred hands.

You one of the roading boys? he says. I'm Don.

Hey. I'm—

Got any ID?

When I get back with the jugs there's a couple of trampers sitting at the end of our table. A story comes on the TV about the Ruatoki police raids, all helicopters and black balaclavas and shouting.

Fucken rubbish, the first tramper says. Eight million bucks of surveillance and they catch some guys shooting pigs in the hills.

More like shooting their mouths off in the pub, his mate says. Cops've been watching too many movies. They reckoned there'd be grenades and napalm, and all they got was three old rifles. Like there'd be Maori terrorist camps in New Zealand.

Taihoa puts down his beer and leans in close. Nah, he says. It's for real.

What is? the first guy says.

The training camps. Cops found nothing 'cause they're stupid. The real guns are buried. My cousin went to that training camp. It was awesome.

The two trampers go real quiet. They glance at each other.

Cops only found the one camp, Taihoa says, but there's heaps. That's why we're down here. Got work on the roading gang so we got an excuse to come to the island and train.

He nods over at a bunch of fishermen at the pool table. Those fellas too. They're hardcore.

What do they teach you? the first guy whispers.

Taihoa glances round, then leans in even closer. It's the al-Qaeda training manual with a Maori flavour. Heavy weapons and explosives, but they throw in some *taiaha* and *haka* and a bit of cannibalism.

The guy sprays his beer all over the table. JJ pretends to look for something under his chair so they can't see his face.

And bushcraft, Taihoa says. When we get the signal we gotta leave the cities and live off the fat of the land. Or the fat of our enemies.

The two guys are staring at Taihoa. Now's my chance.

He's just taking the piss, I say. The real threat is the octopus.

At that the boys lose it. The what? JJ gasps.

The octopus.

Fucken yeah! Taihoa says. You tell 'em. The al-Qaeda terrorist octopus.

I'm serious, I say. There's a giant octopus in the bay. If we make a wrong move and wake him up, we're done. All of us.

The boys are crying with laughter. People are looking at us. Taihoa slides open the heavy sash window and tries to light a cigarette. The wind keeps blowing his matches out. There's a buzzing sound coming from nearby.

Hear that? Taihoa says. They're out there training now. How to use a chainsaw in the dark.

Shut the bloody window! Don the publican yells.

Sure thing, bro, Taihoa yells back. He grabs a full jug off the table and climbs through the window, then closes it behind him. The whole place cracks up. Then the window opens again and Taihoa grins back at us.

C'mon, boys, he says. Bugger the tab.

The boys climb out the window in a sag-arsed tumble, leaving me there by myself. Something goes crunch inside.

Octopus, bitches! I scream through the half-open window. I'm not comin' out. There's a mean-as mother-fucken octopus out there. You better run!

Through the window I see Tama sprawled out under the island's one streetlight. He's fallen over from laughing so hard. Taihoa pulls him up off the gravel and they head towards the wharf. They think the octopus is a helluva joke.

Thing is, I'm not joking.

The boys call me Little Shit. Mostly I'm just Little, when I don't feel like leaving the house. I don't believe anything those days. Other days I'm king of the world and up in your face, I get the full title. Those days I believe too much. Today's one of them. I grab the window and crash it shut. I can't see the boys out on the road anymore. Just the fogged reflection of everybody in the pub staring at me. I turn to face them, breathing hard. I'm still in my dirty work blues and orange high-vis vest.

Crazy bastards, I say. They think I'm takin' the piss.

Nobody moves. They've all stopped talking. There's just the tinny chatter of rugby on the TV and the clink of glasses going down along the bar. Behind the till Don's watching me through slit eyes.

Dad told me to watch for signs out here. We're six days into a summer building roads on Rakiura and I've found one. I step forward into the middle of the room, and start to preach.

Listen up, all right? You fellas gotta be careful out there. When you leave the pub tonight and get in your cars you go in fear, 'cause I saw this huge octopus from the back deck of the launch. Yes, I did. He's sleepin' in the middle of the bay. You piss him off and we're all dead.

I turn to the fishermen round the pool table.

You fellas must have seen him out there on the boats. He's massive.

The nearest fisherman looks at me real hard and gives this little shake of his head, like he's trying to tell me something, but there's no time to ask. The beach is right across the road and the octopus is right there, a black stain spreading under the water. I raise my voice and let it ring out the way Dad does at his sermons.

He's old too. Real old is Te Wheke. He's got a hard-core long memory. He never forgets.

I try to smile but it comes out wrong, all big eyes and teeth like a *pukana* grimace.

Don comes out from behind the bar and walks towards me.

C'mon, nut job, he says. Shut up, pay up and piss off.

There's no hope for this lot. I take a step back. What are you fellas looking at? I ask the room. Don't you know, we're the roading gang. We tried to warn you.

I slide the window back up and half climb, half fall

through it. Outside, the wind tears my clothes off. There's only one thing for it.

Run.


At our place, curled in the dark trying to make myself sleep, I'm safe. But that's not what a leader does. That's not what Dad would do. The others are still out there. I put my boots back on.

It feels like hours before I find them at the wharf. The wind's up and singing through the masts. They've got the back door of the ferry terminal open. JJ's up to his usual shit, banging round inside using his phone as a torch. Taihoa sees me and turns.

Octopus! he yells. Run, you bastard!

Tama cracks up, but then he sees my face. He's got his hood up and his curly afro's coming out the sides. What you on about this octopus, bro? he asks. You havin' a Little Shit day?

Yeah, I tell him. He's somewhere out there, bro. I saw him. Eight arms and a big evil eye. We wake him and we're done. Boom.

I jab Tama in the stomach, harder than I mean to.

Sorry, I say. But it's not safe. We gotta go.

Taihoa frowns. He cocks his head on one side. You're not joking, are you? How you know there's an octopus?

Saw him from the ferry.

How big is he?

I lower my voice. Bigger than the pub.

Tama folds his massive arms. *Riiight*, he says. Bigger than the pub.

I tried to warn those guys but they didn't want to know.

Bugger them, Taihoa says, hopping from foot to foot to keep warm. *Pakeha* get what's coming. But it's all good, right? This octopus isn't gonna come for us?

Waves surge against the wharf below. Taihoa's being nice but I gotta tell the truth. If he gets pissed off, no one's safe, I say.

You're crazy, bro, Taihoa says. He lets that hang there, then his grin flashes white in the dark.

Let's catch him.

My heart bumps.

Tama groans and unfolds his arms. Oh, here we go, he says. For Christ's sake, Taihoa.

Taihoa got his nickname 'cause it means 'cut it out' in Maori. He ignores Tama like he ignores everyone. How 'bout some late-night fishing? he says. We could grab one of these boats.

How we gonna catch a giant octopus? Tama asks through clenched teeth.

Dunno, Taihoa says. He turns to me. Your dad used to catch them, eh? Before he turned all god-freaky?

Seriously, I say, you don't wanna get his attention.

Nah, man, we'd be like Maui. The great ancestor takes his jawbone and tames the sun—we tame the octopus. C'mon.

Before I can say anything he's down the wharf. He stops at a little dinghy at the far end. Aw yeah! Taihoa yells. Late-night fishing is *on*.

While he's untying the ropes, I get this real clear feeling that he's right. We have to go fishing. Dad's always telling us there's a reason for everything, everything for a reason. Tells it to his congregation too, chairs pulled up on the lino in our kitchen on a Sunday morning. He says it so gentle. A reason for everything, everything for a reason. So there's a reason I got kicked out of school and got a job out here, and a reason I saw the octopus. That's the sign. I'm not shit on the end of a shovel today. Over the surf I can hear Dad's voice, clear as.

Watch for signs and you'll know what to do.

I say a prayer under my breath. Lord bless the *pakeha* in the pub who don't want to know, and bless us and the boat, and we'll go do some fishing in your name. *Ko Ihu Karaiti, to matou Ariki, amene.*

All right, I shout. Let's fucken go!


We've just about got the ropes clear when there's a shout from JJ inside the ferry terminal. Check this out, boys!

What is it? Tama calls back.

Just come, dick. Have a look.

We shamble over to the doorway where JJ's standing with this long black bag. He flips it open. By the light of his phone I can see it's a gun case. Three rifles snug in grey foam.

*Shiiit*, Tama says. Where'd you find that?

Locked in the office, JJ says. Must be some hunter going back on the morning launch. There's no bullets, though. They store them separate.

It's another sign. Everything's becoming clear. Sweet as, I say. We can shoot the bastard. I reach into the bag and take a rifle. It feels cold and smooth and good to hold. I point it out to the bay. Bang! Right in his big horny mouth.

Taihoa's grinning like mad. This is his kind of game. He grabs the other rifles, hands one to JJ and keeps one for himself. C'mon, he says. Help me find the bullets.

No way, Tama says. That's heavy shit. Let's just—

We're so busy with the guns that we don't notice the truck pull up till its headlights blaze across us. The doors slam and three huge blokes come marching up the wharf. They're just black shapes against the light. We're too stunned and drunk to move, and in a second I see it's the island's one cop, a heavy Maori guy in a Swanndri and black beanie, and Don from the pub, angry as. Behind them's one of the trampers.

Yeah, that's them, I hear him say.

Shit shit shit, Tama hisses. Put them away—

Oi! a voice booms. What in the hell—

The cop's voice dies when he sees us for real: four scruffy mainlanders, hoods up against the cold, pants slung low, rifles glinting in the yellow glare. I'm still wearing my high-vis vest, lit up in the headlights like an angel. The cop reaches out his hands, palms down, real slow.

What're you boys doing?

I'm still trying to find my tongue when Taihoa starts taking the piss.

It's Tino Rangatiratanga, eh, he says.

Eh? the cop says.

JJ starts giggling.

Time to make the white man *pay*, bro, Taihoa says.

I feel Tama stiffen beside me, mouthing *What the fuck?*

We're the roading gang, I say, stepping forward. We're the four road workers of the apocalypse.

The cop's only metres from us but he turns and runs, grabbing at Don and the tramper on his way past.

Taihoa cracks up. Tino Rangatiratanga! he yells at them, then: Fuck the police, nigger!

In a second they're in the truck and screaming back down the road towards the pub. We just stand there in the growing silence, caught between shit-scared and that mad humour that gets you when you've gone too far.

Time to get the hell out of here, eh boys, Taihoa says. His clean-shaven cheeks are glowing.

Where the hell we gonna go? Tama demands, and our laughter dies. Go hide out at ours? Like they don't know where we live? Only two hundred people on this bloody island.

Man, we're just messing around, JJ says. They know that.

Are we? Taihoa says. Do they?

No, I say. We take the boat and go after the octopus.

There's just the road end, the wharf and the boats. Everything else is a black wall of bush and water. There's nowhere else to go.

We gotta, I say. It's our calling.

Oh, for Christ's sake, Tama says. Let's go—look.

There are lights outside the pub, lights going on in houses up the hill, cars heading our way. We stumble to the end of the wharf and climb down into the boat. JJ and Tama find a couple of orange plastic oars and we push off into the bay. The sound of the waves is the octopus breathing. I cradle the rifle to my chest and hope I'll know what to do. Taihoa's laughing, crouched low in the back of the boat, yelling insults in Maori that the wind snatches away.

Shut up, dick! Tama says. You don't wanna mess with these guys.

The oars aren't doing much, and it takes forever, but once we clear the little point the current takes us out towards the middle of the bay. I look back. Midsummer this far south, there's already faint light in the sky. I can make out cars pulling up beside the Four Square supermarket on the waterfront. They're making a line, blocking off the road down to the wharf. The police truck's red and blue lights pick out figures in the dark, black clothes, the glint of automatic weapons.

A bus comes down the hill and turns towards the wharf. They stop it at gunpoint, and make everybody get off and lie on the ground. I can hear static and feedback in the dawn air. Someone's bellowing into a megaphone and it might as well be in another language. Tama's saying something to me but I can't hear him.

We're getting close now. I can hear the creature stir.

Oi, you okay? Tama says. He shakes my arm.

I open my mouth to crack a joke but nothing comes out. I feel the thunder of long arms running across the ocean floor. We're way out in the bay now, crouched in a rowboat right over the creature's great unblinking eye. The shore's crawling with people, all luring him out. Down on the beach a hunter's dog stands frozen, pointing out to sea, a loud growl of fear in its throat.

I look at the rifle in my hands and I know it's useless. But it's the only jawbone I've got. I know it's my calling, to raise him. I'll raise him up and I'll tame him.

Before anyone can stop me I'm on my feet in the middle of the boat, a luminous orange angel in my high-vis vest. It's the uniform of the reckoning. The uniform of Tino Rangatiratanga. I think of Dad's fierce eyes and I open my arms to the wharf with rifle in hand, towards the lights and the voices and all the people, and I begin to chant.

*Aah-uu-tai-na, ah-hee!*

There's a flare of light. A flare of light and a fierce crack and a huge wind picks us up. Someone cries out and beneath us the surface of the bay explodes. With a roar a blue-black knot of ancient muscle surges up beneath us like a blunt-nosed submarine. He rises. The octopus, the mighty octopus Te Wheke, rises from the boiling sea. Oceans thunder from his back. He rises and we fall, and as I fall my gaze takes in the frightened faces of the hunters and the farmers hunkered down behind their utes.

Eight tentacles go hissing out across the waves—as thick as mighty tree trunks, as thick as mighty *waka* horned with weed and lethal suckers—and the last thing I see before I hit the water, before a tentacle lashes through the front of the pub in an explosion of wood and glass and the gas tanks go up with a thumping flash, before another great arm hurls the police truck through the front of the Four Square, the last thing I see is the gleaming, dripping *moko* carved upon the creature's face and the look in its single world-sized eye that says, finally: it's time.

# MAKING IT

MY CAREER began for real in Manhattan, on an unusually mild winter's evening, with a total fucking scrum. I opened the gallery door and peered out into the street. A huge expectant crowd looked back. There were patrons and buyers and star-fuckers and wannabe artists. I imagined, for one dishonest second, that they were there for me.

My job was to hold the door open. I held the door open.

Oh my god, someone yelled. Here she comes!

The crowd surged forward, shoving and shouting. A phalanx of security guards pushed a beachhead into the fray. Reeves Galleries weren't taking any chances. Goose, golden egg, etcetera.

Next came a huddle of gallery big shots: the director,

two publicists screaming into their phones, the senior curators, plus my bemused girlfriend Lucy, straight from her hospital rounds. In the centre of the huddle, at the centre of everything, was the artist. Katherine DuCroix. Close enough to touch.

Katherine DuCroix was the rebarbative darling of the east-coast art world. Her enormous surreal self-portraits graced some of the most expensive walls on the planet. She'd already gone down in history for the most MacArthur Fellowships (three), and the shortest acceptance speech ('Fools'). She was stout, fierce and a little bit mad: a female Napoleon.

Tonight she wore a pearl silk blouse and heavy black eyeliner, and her wild grey hair was twisted into a bun. She might have been three times my age, but I thought she was beautiful. She looked like she was about to stab the director.

I'm so sorry, he shouted. The cabs should have been here at eight. We'll get to the restaurant soon.

I let the door swing shut and joined Lucy at the back of the pack. To our left a man with long tangled hair lunged through the crowd like a drunken prophet. He strained at a gap between two guards.

Katherine, he yelled. Tell us your secret. How do you do it?

Dude, I yelled, you have to draw with a mechanical pencil.

Nick! The director fixed me with a ball-shrinking glare.

I blushed, but when he turned away I saw Katherine DuCroix looking at me. She seemed amused. My heart gave a squirming flip.

Katherine DuCroix was the reason I wanted to be an artist. There's nothing unusual in that: she inspired a generation. But I was more obsessed than most. Our apartment was wallpapered with prints from her Spirochette series. I'd gone to see all her recent shows, on both coasts. I'd even painted my own versions of her self-portraits, trying to get inside her skin. And there she was, smiling up at me.

Please, the long-haired man cried again. Tell us where your ideas come from.

Move back, a publicist shouted. Give us some room here!

Shut up, Katherine said. Let me answer that.

The publicist looked shocked. Katherine was famous for refusing to take questions, though there were rumours that Reeves didn't let her. I wondered briefly, absurdly, whether the security guards were there to protect the crowd from her.

You want to be an artist? she called out. The crowd could barely see her, she was so short, but her smoke-rough voice carried through the crush. You want to know the secret of my success?

The man stopped pushing against the guards. Yes, he said. His face wore a look of such sincerity that I felt bad for mocking him.

Then shut up, Katherine said, and I'll tell you.

The man fell quiet, and others who had heard the promise fell quiet, and the hush spread through the crowd. Even the guards craned round to listen.

Everyone asks what my secret is, Katherine said. But I never tell the truth, because no one would believe me.

*I'd* believe you, the man offered. There were murmurs of assent.

Well then, Katherine said.

She looked out at the sea of faces. Even the blue-grey air and the traffic gleaming south along Fifth Avenue seemed freighted with expectation. I was pretty sure there was no secret to being an artist, but I realised I wished there was. I was holding my breath as much as anyone when she spoke.

The secret, she said, is syphilis.

There was a short pause. Everyone looked confused.

I stifled a splutter. Then Katherine DuCroix erupted in a furious wheezing cackle, and I let myself go. The sound of our laughter billowed out through the crowd.

Oh my god, Katherine said, turning to me. The look on their faces. I've always wanted to say that.

People will believe anything, I said.

They will, she said. You're cute.

The long-haired man was staring at her, face flushed with humiliation. People around him were laughing, but it was a thin, uneasy sound. Behind us a single cab pulled up.

Here! someone shouted. Katherine. Go.

We were moving again. The security guards cleared a path to the waiting car. I felt Lucy's hand, cool and firm, take mine in the crush. The director held the cab door open. Katherine tugged at my jacket.

You, she said. Jump in this one.

But he's—the director said.

I'm just—I said.

Come on, ride with me, Katherine said. She dragged me into the cab. I let go of Lucy's hand and climbed in. Katherine reached over to shut the door. Lucy climbed in anyway, folding her long legs into the back seat.

She with you? Katherine said.

Yes.

Fine. Shut the door. We'll see you at the restaurant, she yelled out the window. Driver, drive!

We slipped away from the kerb. Behind us, the director was shouting something. All I caught was my name. He didn't look angry. I thought he looked scared.


Not many people got the chance to meet Katherine DuCroix. She lived upstate, and came to maybe one of her openings a year. I'd once overheard a senior curator talking to her on the phone. *Yes. Sorry. Sorry. Yes.* That was all you said to Katherine DuCroix. Her work sold more than the rest of our artists put together. I couldn't believe the warmth against my thigh was coming from *her*.

She slumped in the seat and shut her eyes. Up close, her face was small and round, with a forceful nose and a lemon-twist mouth. Her brows had been plucked into sharp, questioning lines. I'd never seen someone wearing so much make-up.

Oh my god, she said. Fucking people.

You must get those questions a lot, I said.

I do. She opened one eye and looked up at me. What's the secret of anyone's success? Fucking the right curator?

No secret, huh, I ventured. I guess you're just born with it.

Gauguin was born with it, she said. Most people get it later in life. Anyway, where's this damn restaurant?

I don't know, sorry.

Katherine frowned. Why not?

I'm just the intern. We weren't invited to dinner.

Katherine began to laugh with that same wheezing rasp. She didn't sound well. She put a hand on my shoulder. You've just made my night, she said. I could kiss you, whoever you are.

I'm Nick, I said. This is Lucy.

Lucy had come from a twelve-hour shift at the hospital. Her hair was pulled back from her pale freckled face. The two women exchanged a nod.

Good to meet you, Ms DuCroix, Lucy said.

Likewise. It's a damn shame we don't know the name

of that restaurant. I love those fucking dinners. But what do you know? My phone's off. Yours too, right?

Right, I said. I dug my phone from my pocket. Nine missed calls. I switched it off.

Good, Katherine said. I know this great Korean place. Let's go have some fun.

The enormous restaurant had just a few tables, lit up like small, expensive islands. An albino waiter in a black vest led us to a booth up the back. Katherine kicked off her shoes and stepped inside, and I turned briefly to take Lucy's hands. I'd been volunteering at Reeves for years. I'd lose my internship for sure, but dinner with Katherine DuCroix was worth it. I gave Lucy a terrified grin. She seemed exhausted, but she squeezed my hands and managed to smile back.

Inside the booth Katherine was seated cross-legged at a low table. A huge painting hung at her back—a seascape of sorts, wading birds silhouetted against a fiery sunset. I realised it was one of hers. The birds were oilrigs, and the waves at their feet were tiny boats. The water was on fire.

We sat, and a waiter brought pickles and *kimchi*, and a carafe of *soju*. Katherine sloshed the clear spirit into porcelain cups.

So, Nick, she said. You work for a dealer gallery, but you're not a total asshole. Are you an artist yourself?

Well, I said. I want to be a painter.

Really? Katherine said. Someone said that to Lucien Freud at a party once: I want to be a painter. You know what he said? What a coincidence. Neither do I.

No, I really—

A joke, darling. Lucien Freud was diseased and mad. But you have the look of the serious artist about you.

I blushed stupidly. Wow, I said. Really?

Absolutely. I can always tell.

Uh—thanks. Art's what I want to do with my life.

Lucy was looking at me sideways. I guess I'd never stated it like that before.

Well, cheers to that, Katherine said. She raised her cup and drained it in a single gulp, and I did the same.

Of course, you're insane, she said. Wanting to make art in this day and age. There's no future in it.

How can *you* say that? I said.

I'm the exception that proves the rule. It's a lost cause.

I shook my head. I want to make art like you. I love your Spirochette period, and the Paralysis portraits. I've been to about a million of your openings. So, I hope you don't mind me asking, but—is there a secret to your success?

For a second Katherine DuCroix's face was savage: teeth bared, her dark eyes blank with rage.

Then she was off again with that cascading asthmatic laughter. She grinned at me and I grinned back.

You got me, she said.

You got us all back there. Syphilis. Hilarious.

Katherine nodded, and her smile drifted away.

Hilarious, she said, but what if it was true? Some of the great artists had syphilis. Cézanne, Margritte, Yoko Ono.

I wasn't sure whether or not to laugh. Lucy was watching Katherine with a look I couldn't read. She hadn't touched her *soju*.

Didn't it drive them crazy? Lucy asked.

Absolutely, Katherine said. What if it made them brilliant as well?

Lucy lowered her elbows to the table and sat forward. Millions of people got syphilis, she said. Only a few were brilliant. The rest just died.

Katherine leaned in as well, and the two women's faces were close. They all had visions, Katherine said. Maybe they were all brilliant. They just didn't know how to communicate what they saw. A disease can't teach you how to paint.

What a concept, I said. I could use it in my work. Self-portrait with syphilis.

You do self-portraits too? Katherine said. Tell me about them, handsome.

I gulped down another shot of *soju*. I wanted to get this right. They're self-portraits, I said, but they're versions of me that have fallen in love with my own work. So—

Pygmalion? Katherine said.

Pig what?

Shaw had it. Never mind. Go on.

23

So, there's a portrait of me where I'm so obsessed with painting, I've forgotten about the real world. There's another of me after I've lost touch with my friends, and another after Lucy's left me—

You know, Katherine said, I could be the artist in your series.

Wow, I said. You—get caught up in your own work?

No husband, no kids, no friends. All I have is the world on the canvas.

Really?

Really. You have to choose between the real world and the one you're creating.

Wow, I said again. You had to choose between having a family and making art?

Katherine gave a little barking laugh. Not much of a choice, she said. No one would have me. My friends all thought I was nuts. They chose partners and kids, I chose painting. Pretty poor substitute for a nice cock.

Beside me, Lucy was shifting on her cushion like she couldn't get comfortable. I didn't want her interrupting. I reached over and patted her hand.

But it's not really a choice, Lucy said. Most artists have children.

True, Katherine said. Most artists have children. Most artists lead happy lives. Most artists are crap.

But you must lead a happy life, I said. You're so successful.

Hardly, Katherine said, and her face dropped, the weight of the years spilling out. I don't tell anyone this, but I'll tell you. I start from zero every time. Every new show starts out as a failure. I have no idea if it'll be any good.

Wow, I said. That must be tough.

It is, Katherine said. She looked me in the eye. It's very lonely.

Yeah, I said. That must be very hard.

There was a pause. We both drank.

When the waiter returned and Katherine ordered mains, in Korean, Lucy murmured in my ear.

Babe, let's not stay too long.

What? Why not?

She's getting drunk and maudlin. And she wants to fuck your brains out.

What? I whispered. She's older than my mum.

Exactly. It's embarrassing.

We're just talking about art.

Please. You're just stroking each other's egos. I'd rather not sit and watch. And can you stop saying 'wow'?

So, Julie, Katherine butted in. What do you do?

Lucy.

Lucy. What do you do?

I'm a doctor.

A doctor, Katherine said. She poured herself another drink. That could be useful. I have a very good doctor. You know, they found the files belonging to Hitler's doctors.

They think he might have had syphilis. It would explain his insane genius.

What? Lucy said. Are you trying to say the Holocaust was caused by *syphilis*? That's so reductive. Besides, they had antibiotics in the forties. They could have cured him in a week.

Sure, Katherine said. They *could* have cured him, but maybe he didn't let them. Why kill your inspiration? Same for Brett Whiteley and Ralph Hotere. Same for Tracey Emin and the Guerilla Girls. I think they all chose to be diseased. What does that tell you?

You think people wanted that? Lucy said, outraged. It's one of the most painful conditions there is! Why would—

Shush, Katherine said. Here we go.

The waiter—no, the chef himself—swooped down with a covered silver platter. He lifted the lid, and a mushroom cloud of steam billowed towards the ceiling. Beneath, something moved on a bed of seaweed. A dismembered octopus, still twitching.

Fresh meat! Katherine cried.

She stabbed at the pile and came away with a small blue-white tentacle that curled itself round her chopsticks. She shook it off into her mouth and gave a grunt of pleasure. Ungh. Fuck yes. Come on, you two.

I don't know, I said.

Don't be shy, Katherine said. It won't bite.

I forked a slice of tentacle into my mouth. It was

pungent and briny, shivering with escaping life. It was like biting off someone's tongue while French kissing.

Lucy ignored the food. She was staring at Katherine with a look of disgust. So you're telling us a garden-variety STD makes people brilliant? she said. Or is this just some stupid story you feed to—

Lucy, I said. She's just kidding.

You're a doctor, Katherine said. You would want to treat it. But what if you could reap the benefits? What if you could manage it?

Manage it? Lucy said. Manage your face falling off?

Maybe it was worth it.

Paralysis? Psychosis? For the sake of fucking *art*?

The truth! Katherine crowed. Fucking *art*! If you want to make art you have to make sacrifices. You have to choose. Here, Nick, try this one.

She picked out a choice tentacle and offered it across the table, not to my plate but to my mouth. I craned over. She dropped the twitching thing onto my tongue.

Jesus! Lucy said. She leaped to her feet. Her cheeks were spotted with colour. I've had about enough of this. I'm sorry Nick, but she's deranged. We're going.

Katherine was cackling with laughter. She could see I wanted to leave, and Lucy could see I wanted to stay. I sat, foolish with indecision, the octopus jerking in my mouth, until Lucy stormed from the booth. I half rose to go after her.

27

Your girlfriend's right, Katherine said. I am deranged. Blame the disease.

But you're kidding, aren't you? Tell me you're kidding.

You say you want to be an artist, Katherine said. You say you want to know the secret to success. You can run after her now, live a good life, jerk off over the catalogues from other people's MoMA retrospectives, die a nobody. Or you can stay and I'll tell you the truth. Come here.

She stretched across the table and pulled me close. In the gloom her eyes were black, with just the faintest sparkle.

I'll tell you the secret, she whispered. It's not syphilis.

It's not?

No. It's a strain of syphilis. One very rare strain. That's what makes you a genius.

But—

You don't catch it by accident, Katherine said. It's been passed down the generations, artist to artist. You'd be surprised who's got it. But you have to want it badly. It means you'll never have a proper family. You'll never be part of normal society. You have to be prepared to go a bit crazy.

This close, I caught a smell off her, something bitter and strange, and I was sure I could see the ravaged skin beneath her make-up. She raised a hand and caressed my cheek, and I was filled with horrified longing.

You have to be trusted, she said with quiet intensity. Not just anyone gets it. These are the germs that lived in

Louise Bourgeois. This is Dalí in your bloodstream. This is making love to Frida Kahlo. Imagine the things you'd dream. Imagine the things you'd paint. You'd be a genius. Imagine that.

Imagine that, I whispered.

Those who have the disease choose who gets it next, she said. She ran a thick, clammy finger across my lips.

I choose you, she whispered. Fuck me, and it's yours.

# PHOTOCOPY PLANET

JORA CRADLED the book to his chest. He barely saw the rickshaws crammed with school children, or the camels bridled and loaded, or the veiled and laughing women flowing past. Through the dusty market and on up Fort Road he pressed the book close. He muttered to himself as he went.

*This time, please god, this time.*

Jora was charming in English and a ball-breaker in Hindi. He was short and fiery, and dressed like a rich Delhiwallah: a sharp grey suit, purple polo shirt, and small dark glasses that turned clear when he entered the lobby of his hotel. He'd had it built from honeyed sandstone like an old *haveli*. It was five storeys high, with twelve rooms, an open-air rooftop restaurant, and no guests.

His nephew Raj, the tout, stood at the front desk with the day clerks, clustered mindlessly round a radio. They looked up with the faces of men short on sleep and pay. Jora didn't care. They were all family. Without him they'd be hauling bricks in the villages. He brandished the book. It's here, he cried. This time!

The men grinned and left the desk and jostled him up the stairs, and floor by floor the whole staff of nephews and sisters and cousins crowded in behind. When Jora emerged into the restaurant on the roof he felt like a king leading his entourage. He placed the book on a table.

Who will read? he said.

They pushed forward Jora's niece Nisha, a bright bird of a girl still in school. She took the book in her hands like it was a holy text, and leafed through the photocopied pages until she found the spot. A hush fell. The winter sun was clear and bright on her face.

*Lonely Planet India*, she announced in a careful voice. Jaisalmer. Where To Stay. Hotel Rajasthan. Raja's Palace. Sarkar Hotel. Swami Mansions.

Well? Jora said.

Nisha read the listings a second time. She checked the index. She couldn't look at her uncle.

I'm sorry, Uncle-*ji*, she said quietly. Not this year.

All eyes turned to Jora. A sour rage passed through him. He looked past their faces, past the medieval town tumbling down the slope to the desert sands beyond. With the loans he'd taken to build the hotel, they couldn't afford another year of hoping.

He picked up the guidebook. I will get us written into this book, he said.

There were sceptical murmurs.

How? cousin Sunil asked. The book comes from abroad.

The bookwallah said it came from Delhi, Jora replied.

But it's written in England.

Australia, Nisha said.

No, Jora's right, someone said. It's Delhi we need.

It was Raj, the tout. He came forward with his oiled black hair and sharp cowboy boots, and took the book from Jora's hands. These are all photocopies, he said. They come from Delhi.

Then I'll go to Delhi, Jora said. I'll find who prints them and I'll make the sons of bitches put us in their book.

Jora took a bus to Jodhpur station, then fought his way aboard a sleeper for the capital. At four in the morning he woke to a sandstorm blasting through the open-sided carriage. It seemed a bad sign. He'd grown up poor in Bandha, and he couldn't read or write, and he covered his shame by bragging about all three. He was proud that an illiterate man could own a hotel. But how could an illiterate man get himself published in a book? He and his fellow passengers were coated in fine white desert sand.

He wrapped his blanket round his face and drifted into gritty sleep.

Outside Old Delhi Station, Jora hired an auto-rickshaw. He leaned from the open side of the vehicle to scan the road. It was early and freezing. Traffic ghosted through the smoke from last night's rubbish fires.

He found what he sought in Chandni Chowk. An old man unloaded books from the back of his bicycle, and there on his rug was the telltale blue of *Lonely Planet*.

*Baba*, he called. Is your *Lonely Planet* real, or an Indian copy?

The man looked offended. *Sahib*, all my books are real.

Then I don't want it.

Wait. The man carried the book slowly to the rickshaw and put it in Jora's hands. You mean is this book a real *copy*? Then you're in luck, my friend.

Jora smiled. How much?

Sixty rupees.

I'll give you eighty if you tell me where you got it from.

Jora spent the day following the guidebook across Delhi. The old bookwallah bought his copies from a stall in Khan Market, whose owners got them from a back-alley distributor. An hour arguing in the street with the stout Punjabi who ran the place and a small fortune in *baksheesh* got him directions to the warehouse. From there it was a short drive to the factory on the outskirts of Okhla Phase III.

Jora stepped from the rickshaw and gazed up at the building. It was painted the same blue as the guidebooks, and from where he stood it seemed as big as a stadium. The guard waved him through the front gate without question. Jora walked down to the reception past a long line of pristine Mercedes and Audis. The drivers watched him pass.

I'm here to see the manager.

The tall receptionist gave him a sarcastic smile. I'm sure you are, sir. They're about to start. Good luck.

She pressed a button and the door at her back clicked open. Jora had no idea what she was talking about. He gave her a curt nod and went straight through, into a lobby with a strangely low ceiling and an elevator set in one wall. He chose the top floor. If he were manager, that's where his office would be.

He was staring at his tired face in the polished steel doors when they slid open. His reflection split in half to reveal a metal gangway suspended above an enormous factory floor. A vaulted ironwork ceiling arched overhead.

Jora moved to the edge of the gangway and gripped the railing. Far below, rows of battered photocopiers, thousands of them, stretched off into the distance. An army of workers in blue overalls loaded cartridges and paper, or stood conversing in tight groups. The bustle called to mind a great railway station.

You there! a rich, fruity voice cried. Last bets.

Jora turned to see a small crowd gathered further

along the walkway. They were drinking champagne and watching the preparations below. A man with a formidable moustache strode towards him. He had the same short stocky build as Jora, and when they were face to face Jora saw they wore identical glasses.

I have business with the manager, Jora said.

The man looked him up and down and paused, as if making a decision, then gave a small formal bow.

I am the manager, he said. Business must wait. Any last bets?

What are we betting on? Jora asked.

We are betting on the copying of the *Lonely Planet* guide. Where are you from?

I grew up in the poorest village in Rajasthan. But now I'm—

Yes, the manager cut him off. You look like a village man. Which one?

Jora stiffened. Jaisalmer will do.

Jaisalmer it is. You are betting on page two hundred and twelve. Minimum bet five hundred rupees.

Jora took his wallet and casually counted out ten thousand rupees. It was far more than he could afford. He had just enough left for the train home.

The manager took the money and made a note in his book. Then he turned to the railing and pointed down to a group of workers in the vivid red turbans of Jaisalmer men.

That is your row, the manager said. They have never

won. Now, let us begin. He leaned over the railing and clapped his hands.

An air-raid siren filled the factory. The workers below rushed into a vast and swirling choreography, as intricate as a North Korean spectacular. Chaos resolved itself into row upon perfect row, a worker standing to attention at each machine. Jora watched transfixed. Around him the betting crowd moved to the railing.

At the end of the factory an official made his way across the floor. He stopped at the first copier in each row and handed its operator a white envelope.

The originals, the manager said. Each row gets one page from the original guidebook to copy. Three hundred pages, three hundred rows.

Once the envelopes were distributed a hush fell. The workers and the crowd fixed their total attention on the manager. He raised both arms above his head, then brought them swiftly down.

Go!

The little crowd roared, and at the start of each row the workers tore open their envelopes and thrust the precious originals into their machines. A mighty whirring clamour filled the factory like a flock of mechanical pigeons taking flight, and a jagged line of light flared across the roof. Jora raised a hand to shield his eyes.

The first copies rolled from the machines; as in a baton race the next worker in each row seized the duplicate and fed it into his machine and made a copy, which was in turn taken up and copied by the next and so on, passing copies of copies of copies down the factory in a furious relay.

The race passed beneath Jora's feet and away to the south, where the machines were old and decrepit and soon began to choke and jam. The stench of toner filled the air. Repair teams raced along the rows, vanishing and reappearing amid the steam and smoke. The strobing line of light that marked the progress of the race grew ragged as some rows fell behind and others surged ahead.

At the front, the Jaisalmer row was neck and neck with a sleek Delhi team. Jora found himself gripping the rail and urging his desert cousins on.

Go, you sons of bitches!

At that, a woman leaned over the railing to cheer the Delhi team. She thrust one slender arm into the air, spilling champagne from her glass. The golden liquid, seemingly an extension of her glittering sari, rained down upon the last copier in the Delhi line. The machine stuttered and sizzled. The operator stumbled back. Across the floor Jaisalmer forged ahead. Their final machine spat out the final copy and the turbanned workers threw up their arms in victory.

A win, cried the manager, a surprise win for two hundred and twelve!

Jora cheered until he was hoarse. A Jaisalmer worker held up the final copy for all to see. It looked completely blank.

When the noise died down the manager held out his hands. Ladies and gentlemen, that concludes the fifty-second copying of *Lonely Planet India*. The floor will now be closed for collation and binding. We will see you all next month.

He turned to Jora, his mouth a thin displeased line. Follow me.

At the end of the walkway the manager entered an office lined with oak. Framed first editions of *Lonely Planet India* hung around the walls. He sat at his desk, unlocked a drawer and counted out a very large sum of money. He shoved this across the table to Jora.

So, the manager said. Business.

Jora ignored the money. He was feeling good. He crossed one leg over the other and said, I want to change the guidebook.

The manager smiled. Impossible, he replied.

Jora said nothing. He let the silence grow.

What do you want to change, the manager said, irritated.

I want my hotel listed.

Impossible, the manager repeated. If I change the guidebook it is no longer the guidebook. No one will buy a copy if it differs from the original.

But they're already different. Those last copies are blank.

Those we sell in the villages. The further from Delhi, the worse the copy. But this a problem of technology, not intention. If I could make every copy perfect, I would.

All I ask is one small addition. Here.

Jora passed a crumpled slip of paper across the manager's desk. Grains of sand spilled onto the dark wood. The manager took the paper, then swept his sleeve across the desk. He began to read.

But this is a fantasy, he said. I am sure you would like your hotel to have *the best food in Rajasthan*. You wish it to be so, but your desire does not make it so.

But it's the honest truth.

Perhaps. But it would be dishonest of me to make this change.

You think you're honest, copying someone else's book?

The copies I make are honest to the original.

But are they honest to India? How, if they don't include my hotel?

Ask the editors of *Lonely Planet*.

It's a tiny addition. Two lines of text.

Do you see two lines of empty space waiting for you? Go back to your village. India is full.

Jora clasped the stacks of thousand-rupee notes and slid the money back towards the manager. India is never full, he said.

The manager's nostrils flared. He gripped the arms of his chair and sat forward. Listen, *choot*. You are an illiterate village dog. I have been to the West. I know what these people want, and I will stay true to their vision. They are not interested in yours.

Jora stood and scooped the cash into his bag. I am a village man, he said, and you are an uncle-fucking pirate and a fool. Put me in your book!

The manager rose to his feet, and the two short men stood glaring at each other.

Out of the question, the manager shouted. Now get out of my office!


Jora spent the seventeen-hour journey home in a fury. He railed against the manager and the sons of daughters of camels who had fathered him. Yet, hour by hour, the steady weight of the bag in his lap calmed him down. There was enough in there to pay off much of his debt. But he wouldn't pay off his debt. When he stepped from the bus into the freezing sands of Jaisalmer, he knew what he would do instead.

Sir, you need a hotel? a tout called out to him. Shahi Palace! Very good write-up in *Lonely Planet*!

It was his nephew Raj, sitting at Shinde's chai stall. Jora sat and called for tea, and handed Raj the bag.

Feel that, he said.

What's in there?

About ten *lakh* cash.

Raj laughed and weighed the bag in his hand. Books, *na*? How many copies did you get changed?

Have a look.

Raj opened the bag and went still. He looked up at his uncle, then back down into the bag. What is—he said. How is this—

That's for you, Jora said. I want you to buy every photocopier in Rajasthan.

Raj and his brothers' battered yellow Maruti became a familiar sight, trundling back and forth with copiers strapped to the roof. In a month they acquired enough machines to fill a derelict tannery. The north wall was half buried beneath sand blown in from the desert, but the rent was cheap.

Next Jora went to his brothers in the restaurant kitchen. He laid an original *Lonely Planet* on the chopping block. Sharpen your knives, he said. Imagine you are cutting a diamond.

His brothers went to work on the binding, slicing out each page.

Then Jora sat down with his niece Nisha. Your ignorant uncle can't read or write, he said. How'd you like to do it for me?

In the mornings and after school Nisha studied the guidebook. Then she carefully composed a paragraph about Shahi Palace on the hotel's antiquated laptop, and pasted it over the entry for Sarkar Mansions. It was hard to tell that it wasn't part of the original.

On the morning of the first printing Jora closed the hotel and assembled his staff at the tannery. It was the dead of winter and there were no guests. Jora issued instructions, his breath fogging in the cold, and there were questions and laughter and barking dogs, but soon enough everyone stood ready. Though there would be no race, Jora couldn't help himself. He raised his arms, and brought them swiftly down.

Go!

When the copies were made and the bindings done and the books stacked in the hotel lobby, Jora was proud. He took one and thumbed through it. They were rough: pages were upside down or missing, and in his copy someone had swapped the entry on Shimla for a photograph of Kabir Bedi in very small shorts. But to Jora, who could not read and could not write, they were perfect. He was in there. His family, his hotel, his life.

He snapped the book shut and turned to the desk. Raj, he called. Have you been to the city before?

All the time.

Jora laughed. Not Jodhpur. How'd you like to go to Delhi? On my money?

Raj attempted a shrug. Then he broke into an enormous smile.

You take these to Delhi, Jora said, and you don't come back until you've sold every last one.

Two days after the family had seen Raj and Sunil off from the bus station, the boys were back. Sunil's arm was broken. Raj's handsome face was an ugly pulp.

We set up at Old Delhi, Raj said through swollen lips. We were only there a day and these five men came up to us and said it was their corner. You know what the bastards said? Fuck off back to your village. India is full.

Jora hurled his drink off the balcony. That dog, he cried. India is never full! What about the books?

Raj dropped his gaze. I'm sorry, Uncle-*ji*.

Jora spent the days shouting at his waiters, and the nights drinking Old Monk by himself in the restaurant. He'd spent everything. There was no more money for toner or paper. There were few guests and no books. All he had was a sand-strewn room full of ancient photocopiers, and crushing debt.

India, he told his glass, is empty.

One morning Nisha came to see him.

Why aren't you at school? he asked.

Nisha handed him a sheet of paper. I made this for you, Uncle-*ji*.

It was the main Jaisalmer page from the guidebook, except that Nisha had pasted new paragraphs over the entire text, and replaced the photographs with hand-drawn pictures. It looked like a school assignment.

That's lovely, Jora said. I'll put it on the wall in my office.

No, Nisha said, pointing to the new paragraphs. That's Sunil's camel treks, and that's the taxi drivers, and that's the laundry service on Fort Road.

But they're not in the guide, Jora said. Why would we put them in the—

Jora went door to door. He asked his friends and neighbours if they wanted to appear in a new edition of *Lonely Planet*. He sat cross-legged in their homes and invented prices according to the sweetness of their tea. He charged the shawl sellers in the old fort one hundred rupees for a listing. Srinagar's Jewellers paid two thousand. Nisha wrote the entries and pasted them in, and if a business wanted a photo but didn't have one, she drew them a picture. In a month they had enough money to buy paper.

This time the printing was quicker, but sales were slower than the Jodhpur bus. Local bookwallahs shook their heads and pointed to their existing stock, and Jora didn't dare send anyone back to the capital. The few copies Raj sold at the bus station made little difference to bookings at the hotel.

The only vendor Jora could find who didn't seem to stock *Lonely Planet* was in the waiting room at Jodhpur Station. The gap-toothed old Marxist who ran the stall was always busy. People came to sit and argue politics with him, and most left with a book under their arm. Jora studied his wares and then approached.

Do you have *Lonely Planet India*? he asked.

No sir. Imperialist trash. What I have is this.

The man pulled a foxed volume from the bottom of a pile. This is the only guide to India you'll ever need.

Jora studied the faded red cover. The characters seemed more unfamiliar than usual. What language is this? he asked.

Russian. Hotels all approved for their socialist values. This is the latest edition. Nineteen sixty-six.

Listen, *baba*, Jora said. How would you like to sell an up-to-date, um, socialist version of *Lonely Planet*?

The man jumped to his feet. Does such a thing exist?

Jora pulled the guide from his bag. See here, he said. Everyone's listed. No one is turned away. I'll give them to you very cheap.

The man took the book and flicked through. He paused at Kabir Bedi's tiny shorts.

And I'll feature your stall in the next edition, Jora said.

The man's eyes gleamed. You would put *me* in *Lonely Planet*? he asked.

For free.

The bookwallah smiled. He had a mischievous gap between his *paan*-stained incisors. I can sell these, he said. How many have you got?

The Jodhpur bookwallah pressed copies on every tourist coming through the station. His whole family was in the book trade, and within a month the guide was displayed in markets and bazaars across the city. The vendors bragged to friends that they themselves would appear in the next edition, and by the end of winter the second printing was nearly sold out. Bookings at the hotel slowly rose.

With the change in seasons the heat began to build. Nisha stayed home from school, working beneath the turning fans to add the new material. Word had spread far beyond the bookwallahs that it was now possible for anyone to get themselves listed in *Lonely Planet*. Jora held court in the rooftop restaurant. Officials from the surrounding *panchayats* climbed the stairs to beg for the inclusion of their villages. Wealthy families had their weddings and mansions written in. For a handful of coins even the fruit vendors who lined the market could have their work praised in the guide.

There is always room, Jora cried. India is never full!

The tannery blazed with the light of photocopiers long into each night. They went through a third printing, and then a fourth, and with each new addition the book became more idiosyncratic. Nisha grew tired of imitating the guide's original style. Her entries began to sound like a studious thirteen-year-old Rajastani girl, and when she could no longer keep pace with new additions, people were allowed to write their own.

The fonts grew wildly mixed. Hinglish and Bengali and hyperbole crept in. People supplied their own skewed maps that placed themselves at the centre of their city or town. They spoke of how their broadband was as fast as light, their railways faster still. They wrote of how their *lassi* prolonged life, how the women of their town had the finest minds and fiercest gods. The book grew to six hundred pages.

By the fifth printing, no tourist could mistake the book for the real thing, or even a copy of the real thing, but many bought it just the same. Jora's guide had a unique, combative vitality. There were five entries for Kolkata, each funded by a rival politician, and each more baroque and outrageous than the last. A string of hypothetical megacities and dams appeared as peaceful realities. There was a bidding war between slumlords and NGOs to write up the nation's slums. People airbrushed their children's faces and Photoshopped their sunsets.

Tourists began travelling to India expressly to take a holiday based on Jora's *Lonely Planet*. To follow it was to give yourself over to chance, to navigate the present with a map of the future. The book had become a thing of pure, virulent aspiration: a guide to the what the country wished and hoped to be.

To mark the printing of twenty thousand books, Jora bought a bottle of well-aged Laphroaig, and a cheap bottle of locally made 100 Pipers. He sat with his extended family in the rooftop restaurant looking over the desert.

The horizon was dotted with campfires: camel traders journeying east to the fair at Pushkar. Jora poured a round of 100 Pipers.

A toast, he said. We're on our way to putting a bunch of filthy village dogs on the map. At the end of the week we'll have paid off one-fifth of our debt.

They laughed and drank until the distant campfires had burned down, and when the 100 Pipers bottle stood empty Jora took it to his office and refilled it with Laphroaig. The next day, hungover and grinning, he took a copy of his guidebook and signed the title page with a crude X. Then he posted it, along with the whisky, to the factory manager in Delhi.

With the onset of another winter, sales died away like the monsoon winds. Each morning Jora entered the lobby to more precarious piles of unsold books. By day he laughed it off. But by night he woke to barking dogs and the fuzzy thump of village weddings, and he knew something had changed. He and Raj took the bus to Jodhpur.

What's going on? Jora asked the Marxist bookwallah. Why doesn't anyone want our book anymore?

They all want it, the man said. The problem is they've already got it.

Jora and Raj walked the streets. The old Marxist was right: every stall had copies of their guide. Children darted out to sell them at traffic lights. They were even in the window of the Oxford Bookstore on Gandhi Marg.

A week later a tall woman with blond ringlets and a shabby man in fake Ray-Bans came into the hotel restaurant, carrying a copy of Jora's guide. They looked around at the sweeping view over the desert.

They were right, the man said. This place is a-*mazing*.

And that must be Jora, the woman said, glancing at the guidebook. Hey, she called. Your place is a-*mazing*.

Thank you, Jora said, beaming. Please, join me.

The couple sat and spread their things across his table. While they moaned about rickshaw drivers, Jora found himself gazing at their guidebook. There was something about it. He picked it up. May I?

Jora read the book the only way he could. He weighed it in his hands. He sniffed it. He tested the paper between finger and thumb. It felt odd, though he couldn't say why. He flicked to the photo section, and his own image stared back, vivid and bright-eyed. It was definitely his guidebook, and yet—

He stood sharply, his *thali* tray crashing to the ground. This is a forgery! he cried.

The couple stared up at him. Jora brandished the book.

You, he demanded. Where did you get this?

But he already knew the answer. He opened the book. Inside the cover, included in the printing itself, was his own scrawled X.

The giant factory in Okhla III. The manager. That bastard was smarter than he looked.

At dusk Jora assembled his brothers and nephews and cousins at the bus stop. They stood wreathed in blankets, and carried cricket bats and bags of *roti* and *chana dal*. In the dim winter monochrome they looked like a mongrel cricket team about to go on tour. Jora went among the men and counted heads.

Thirty, he told the frightened driver.

Please, *sahib*, no trouble, the man said. Is it a family feud? A matter of love?

No, Jora said, a matter of theft.

From Jodhpur the mob took a sleeper to Delhi. They stayed awake singing and smoking *bidis* to hide their nerves. Raj and Sunil bragged about how many copiers they would smash. Other passengers entering the carriage turned and left with eyes averted.

In Delhi the next morning a convoy of rickshaws ferried them south. Most had never been to Delhi before. The desert men gripped their bats and stared out at the gleaming boutiques and chain stores of South Extension. It was too loud and cold to talk above the engines.

At Okhla III they piled out to stand in the factory's shadow.

Follow me, Jora yelled. He marched towards the

guard post with his bat held in both hands.

There was nobody there. The post was unmanned and the gates stood open. They stormed down to the reception shoulder to shoulder. There was no sign of the receptionist, and Jora simply walked around her desk and buzzed them through.

Ten of them pushed into the elevator, packed close with the smell of sweat and smoke. Jora could hardly bear to stand still. No Delhi *choot* stole from him and his family.

The doors slid apart and the men piled out. The cavernous expanse of the factory opened before them. Jora had no time for the spectacle. He turned towards the manager's office.

Halfway along the metal gangway, hunched over the railing, staring vacantly across the factory floor, was the manager himself.

You, Jora said, pointing his cricket bat at the man's head. You're copying my guidebooks.

*Accha*, the manager said, blinking angrily. The beggar returns a publisher. Only an illiterate man could make such a monstrous book.

And only a goat-licking cripple would copy it.

You are right, the manager said. He spat over the side of the railing. I prefer to copy nothing at all.

Jora frowned.

The manager jerked his head. See for yourself.

For the first time Jora noticed the vast factory floor

in disarray below. The copiers had burned to lumps of scorched plastic, or been scavenged for parts, leaving just their carcasses in scattered rows. The breeze from an open fire escape blew tumbleweeds of paper down the empty aisles.

What the hell happened? Jora asked.

You happened, you son of a bitch, the manager said. You ruined me.

But you were copying my books!

I refused to copy your filth. I kept on with the official guide, but soon enough I could barely sell fifty a week. Everyone wanted yours.

But—

You bankrupted me. They're throwing me out.

Jora studied the manager more closely. Gone was the proud bearing. Deep shadows ringed his eyes, and his suit was filthy and stained.

So who *is* copying my book? Jora demanded.

The manager laughed, an exhausted bleat. Does it matter? Your hotel is full, isn't it?

Tell me!

All right then, the manager said bitterly. It's *Lonely Planet*. The real *Lonely Planet*. They've given up on their own guide. Now the bastards just copy yours.

# RUSH

THERE ARE five of them crammed into a white council ute, speeding through the waking city. Jackhammers and shovels rattle in the tray. The young guys in the back are knee to knee in work pants and steel-capped boots. One of them slugs at a Farmers Union iced coffee. It's a Monday morning in Melbourne and just past dawn. Sunlight ripples bronze across the high rises, licks out from laneways in golden tongues.

Big Toff's driving. He's a reassuring bulk up there in the front, not even forty but big and dark and weathered. His massive shoulders protrude from either side of his seat. Next to him, Archie looks tiny. The old man's barely five foot and all sinew, wired tight like an old-time bantam-weight boxer. He riffles the paperwork with tattooed hands, one last time. His scowl is cast-iron with concentration.

Relax, Uncle, Toff says. He speaks with the sharp, tumbling cadences of the Western Desert. You can't beat 'em?

Archie looks up and cracks a grin, and puts the papers back in the glove box.

Past the CBD, Toff swings the ute off St Kilda Road into the cool green of Kings Domain. They crawl along the triumphal avenue with hazard lights winking, and on up to the Shrine of Remembrance. The blunt stone monument squats above the city like a misplaced Greek temple.

Toff parks on the forecourt next to three other council utes. One's got a small excavator on the back. The shrine's grey stone is a confusion of workers in high-vis vests, setting up a safety perimeter. A hard-case woman in mirror shades hammers a white planning sign into the lawn.

Archie climbs down from the cab, and jams a foreman's hardhat over his wiry grey hair. He looks out across the glass spires of the city skyline, as if appraising their value. Then he looks up at the shrine.

All right, you mob, Archie calls. Let's get to work!


By the time the police arrive the paved forecourt and wide granite steps are a mess of smashed rock. The excavator has piled the debris to one side, where a team of workers sift the dirt with wire-mesh pans. A small crowd of onlookers has gathered at the safety perimeter.

A police cruiser pulls in beside the utes. Archie's shoulders hunch tight. Toff drops his sledgehammer and walks quickly over.

Let me, he says.

A sergeant and a constable step from the car. They look like they're at the tail end of a long night shift, their faces creased and tired.

You with the council? the sergeant shouts. The percussion of jackhammers is relentless.

Yeah, Toff yells.

You the boss?

I'm the spokesman.

The policeman cups a hand to his ear. What?

I'm the spokesman!

Huh?

You got a nice tan! Hang on. Toff signals the others to stop work, and soon a dusty silence falls over the Domain. What's the problem?

We had reports of someone vandalising the shrine. But you're council, right?

Right, Toff says.

What're you doing? Maintenance?

Not quite. Here. Toff points to the planning sign. He folds his thick arms across his chest and waits with a half smile.

The sergeant leans down and reads. His weary, businesslike expression ruptures with surprise. He looks at Toff.

You serious?

Deadly.

Mineral Exploration Licence?

You got it. G-two-eighty. Eight weeks, eighty metres down, mining lease if we hit pay dirt.

Pay dirt? You mean you're digging for—

Toff grins. Gold.

The sergeant runs a hand along his stubbled jaw. Right, he says. Gold. This is kind of unusual. You got any paperwork?

Sure, Toff says. I got a twenty-seven-F, all the back checks, an ECB and two double-o-fours. You want them all?

The sergeant shrugs. Toff ducks his bulk under the safety tape and retrieves the papers from the ute. The sergeant reads in silence.

Hang on a minute, he says. *Land* Council? You're from the *Aboriginal Land* Council? He looks sharply at Toff and the work gang at his back. Is this some kind of stunt?

A small, mostly elderly crowd has drifted closer to listen. An unusually tall old man in a blue blazer, a red poppy pinned to his lapel, hovers behind the sergeant. He radiates distress like an old-fashioned bar heater. Activists, the man moans. They're activists.

Toff's amber eyes are trenched deep in his fleshy face, but they're shining. He's been waiting for this. He laughs. *Were* activists, he says. Now we're the Aboriginal

Land Council—of *Minerals*.

The sergeant shakes his head. What's your point? he says. What are your demands?

No demands, Toff says. This isn't a protest action. You know what they say—if you can't beat 'em? He smiles and shrugs. Now we're a real-deal mining company.

The sergeant stares at him and, for the first time in his life, Toff feels the sweet righteousness of bureaucracy rising up in him. This is totally legit, he says. Call the Department of Crown Lands. The number's on the forms.

The sergeant looks sceptical, but he pulls out his phone and dials the number anyway. He is put on hold. After a long wait, a bored operator comes on the line. The sergeant paces while he talks, one hand shading his eyes from the glare.

Who the hell signed off on—okay. Sorry. Sure, the paperwork. Twenty-seven-F? Yep. Two double-o-fours? Two of them, got it. Yes. What? How much to look it up? Jesus! And where'd they get that kind of money? No, it's not a set of GPS co-ordinates, it's the Shrine of bloody Remembrance. No, that is not fascinating. It's—*what*? A typo? It's a fucking typo? The what? Online complaint form? Wait—

The sergeant glares at his phone in frustration.

See, Archie calls, a challenge in his voice. The old man approaches, the high-vis vest around his shoulders like a modern possum-skin cloak. All paid up, he says. We've got a *permit* to do this. Your laws, mate, so you're with us on this one.

Permits can be revoked, the sergeant says. Who are you?

Archie Ryan. I'm the CEO.

Wait a minute, the sergeant says. I know you. You're a serial protester. You're at everything. Any cause that'll have you.

Toff puts a restraining hand on Archie's shoulder, and when the old man speaks his voice is weary and tight.

We're done with protesting, he says. No one gives a shit about land rights in this country anymore. This is a commercial mining operation. You need an injunction to stop it. C-two-forty, federal, with underwritten DCBs. Takes weeks to get and easy as piss to overturn. While you're waiting you could keep that mob under control. They've been threatening my crew.

Damn right we have, the tall old man says. He steps forward and grips the thin safety cordon. His anger seems equal to that of Archie. Why do you have to dig here? he says. Men fought and died for this country. Why the bloody hell would you mine this?

Mate, Archie says with a sour grin, we're hardly going to fuck with our own land.

The city explodes. News crews and photographers and lawyers scramble. The airwaves burn with confused outrage. The Institute of Public Affairs is spotted plagiarising

Wilderness Society press releases, and vice versa. Rio Tinto and Fortescue come out in support of the dig, and the internet is soon awash with rumours of a joint venture to open-cut mine the MCG. Only Tony Abbott distinguishes himself, giving an apparently incoherent yet tactically brilliant speech wherein he coins the slogan 'Support all the Diggers, all the time, whatever they're digging.'

At Kings Domain the crowd swells throughout the afternoon. The workers douse the Sacred Flame with a Kmart fire extinguisher. From behind the police line Toff and Archie watch gleaming charter buses disgorge a flow of pensioners, ferried in from suburban RSL clubs. The protesters carry hand scrawled placards, bags of knitting and glad-wrapped sandwiches. They surge up the hill in a blue-rinsed wave.

Mixed with the elderly crowd is a steady stream of sympathetic locals, students and activists. Away to the east, the youth wing of Socialist Alliance is digging a solidarity hole in the lawn.

A nuggetty man with tattooed arms pushes to the front of the crowd. He's wearing a sticker-covered hardhat and carries an enormous red flag. Orrite, lads, he calls in a broad Scottish accent. We come to show solidarity. This is a bloody good action.

Piss off, mate, Archie says. This isn't an action.

Ha, the man says. Tha's a good line. That'll confuse the hell out the bosses.

I'm serious, you little cunt, Archie says. This is a commercial mining operation. You can't co-opt this. Piss off.

The man's face darkens. We took a vote, he says. The rank and file unanimously voted t' support your action. Why'd you turn that down?

Sorry, mate, Toff says. Us bosses got a press conference to do.

The news crews have been allowed inside the cordon. A big PA has been set up so the crowd can hear. Toff gives Archie the thumbs up.

Go for it, Uncle, he says. Stick to the script, don't lose your cool, eh?

Archie nods. All right, you bastards, he mutters. Let's do this.

After years of speaking to polite but indifferent crowds at other people's rallies, the old man's restless, wary features take on a cast of authority. He seats himself before the bank of cameras, takes out his notes and pulls the microphone close. Over the gunfire rattle of jackhammers, his voice echoes across the Domain.

Afternoon. I'm Archie Ryan. I'm a Wurundjeri man, and CEO of the Aboriginal Land Council—of Minerals. Today is the first day of work at the Kings Domain mine. We have every confidence this mine will yield significant quantities of gold.

There are cries of *Shame!* Signs reading HANDS OFF HALLOWED GROUND bob above the crowd. The tall elderly veteran has made it past the police line, claiming he is feeling faint. He sits against Toff's ute as if resting, then reaches a bony arm under the chassis and handcuffs himself to the vehicle. There are angry shouts and he is swarmed by police.

It is clear, Archie continues, that local people will support this mine, because it brings jobs and money to the local economy. Stand back a minute, would you.

The work crew has chipped out the base of the cenotaph with a jackhammer, as if notching a tree for felling. There is a cry of *Timberrr!* and the mighty stone spear tips slowly forward, then thunders to the ground. The now-huge crowd shrinks back in fright. *You're dead! You're fucking dead*, screams a voice from in the crush.

Now, Archie says, we understand that there are concerns from old soldiers. We have consulted and listened to their concerns. Watching TV and visiting RSLs has taught me the fundamental value of respect for veterans. Listen.

A pre-recorded clip of an RSL consultation meeting booms across the Domain. Over the insane chirping of pokies comes a scrum of angry voices, the thump and squeal of feedback as someone tries to grab the mic. There is shouting, and the terrible splintering sound of dentures crushed underfoot.

I deeply respect old soldiers, Archie continues. There is no ripping-off here. The more time I spend with them, the more I consider myself their true friend. We recognise they have a long history and a rich culture.

The police line tightens as the crowd surges forward in anger. The superintendent watches the mob's every move, his radio at the ready. Archie pushes on. He's enjoying himself now.

We recognise veterans have a long history, but the sad reality is that this memorial was built to commemorate soldiers who are all dead. None of them actually use the shrine. It is a dying culture, and this mine will help to preserve it. Once we have dynamited the structure, we will donate fragments of rock to the museum. We will plant two large trees to commemorate the diggers' sacrifice, at our own expense. Most important of all, we will offer work in the mine to any able-bodied veteran. As we have learned, it is better to work for, rather than against, the mining industry.

The crowd roars its disapproval over the grunt and wheeze of the excavator. Archie's crew works on in the background. From time to time one of them rises from the fast-expanding mineshaft, nervously scans the crowd, then bobs back out of sight.

Archie's nasal voice booms out over the PA. We also offer compensation to veterans. We offer point-zero-six per cent of turnover, shared among all veterans who can prove an unbroken link to this hillock since seventeen eighty-eight. This will be about six dollars each, and will rise even further once gold is found. We trust this generous offer will be looked upon with gratitude.

This time the bellow of anger from the crowd is a

physical force. The police have drawn their batons and fixed their visors. The light is beginning to fade, and shadows pool in the shaft where the workers tunnel beneath the shrine. Up the front a TV technician switches on a bank of halogens. Archie's tense form is a sudden island of light among the seething mass of protesters. He begins to wind up his speech.

We look forward to working with the old soldiers of Victoria, contributing to the wealth of the nation, and making a meaningful living for ourselves, like you've always wanted. Thanks—and if you don't mind me saying, go fuck yourselves.

The crowd erupts. The noise is catastrophic. The police line stumbles back under the onslaught. Two-dozen police horses thunder into action, charging the crowd from either side. There are screams as pensioners go down beneath the hoofs.

Toff moves to Archie's side and it is just the two of them standing in the light, the focus of the crowd's rage.

Shit, Toff says. We have to call this off. Look.

To their right a mass of burly men with crew cuts shoulder-charge the police line. They look like off-duty soldiers. Old-timers beat the police back with their crutches and walking frames. A catheter bag slices the air above Toff's head.

Toff looks back, afraid for the work gang's safety. They have emerged from the mouth of the diggings in a tight high-vis huddle and are shouting to him. He can't hear them over the noise. They move slowly towards Toff and Archie and the brilliant halogen lights.

From the opposite direction the soldiers lead the charge, bellowing and pushing at the cops. Somewhere in the back a furious martial drumming starts up. The police line disintegrates. The crowd is upon them.

They all reach the spotlight at the same instant. As the work gang enters the light, the halogens' fierce rays catch their vests as if catching a huge mirror ball, and the enraged crowd rears back.

Toff realises the workers are moving in a phalanx because they are carrying something enormous. They lower the object carefully to the ground at Archie's feet, then peel away. There is a hot, sharp intake of breath: first from the old man, then the cops, soldiers and pensioners, and those watching live on TV across the country.

It is a gleaming slab of crystalline white quartz, prized from the earth beneath the shrine. And running through it, like a bolt of lightning frozen into the rock, is a seam of gold, as thick as Toff's enormous thigh. Half a million bucks' worth, at least.

For one brief moment the crowd stands in silent awe, and in that glittering pause, a microsecond before the Melbourne Rush begins, each of them feels the ripe slink of blood in their veins, and something else too, something huge and fierce, welling up inside.

# SCAR

## 1

FAR BELOW the plane, the valley's one road twisted through the scrub, an umbilical cord of raw red dirt. It was old goldrush territory down there, broken and remade by hand. From the Cessna's tiny window I watched our shadow dip and loom across the hills' corrupted flanks. Then I saw it—the long dark slash of the mine. I'd studied the surveyor's drawings, but from the air it looked different. The line of the cut was flanked on either side by three clearings, six in all. There was something familiar to that symmetry. I rolled the sleeve of my shirt and turned my arm to expose the veins.

Look, I shouted over the engines.

Christie lowered her pregnancy book. I pointed to the faded scar on the inside of my elbow. It was a pale line flanked on either side by three small punctures, where the doctor had fumbled the stitches almost fifty years ago.

Christie frowned behind her sunglasses. I beckoned her to the window, and she leaned across me to look. I caught her youthful scent, ripe with sweat, and I was glad I'd asked her to come. It was a work trip, a long one. We were trying for a child.

Do you see that? I yelled in her ear.

She looked out at the mine's pattern on the land, then back at my scar. Strange, she yelled. What do you think it means?

Nothing. Coincidence.

How'd you get it?

School. Going down a slide. Bolt.

I mimed the head of the rusty bolt slicing the vein. Christie pulled a face.

Buckle up, the pilot shouted. Here we go.

The plane sank down among the treetops. We bumped along the landing paddock and came to rest beside a dusty LandCruiser. The pilot opened the hatch and folded out the steps, and the warm drone of the bush flooded in. Christie tied back her tangled black hair. She stepped down and stretched, and my eyes grazed the smooth olive jut of her hips where her top rode up. Behind his mirrored aviators the pilot was staring as well. He'd been flirting all day, trying to guess: was she part Spanish or Aboriginal or what?

There's no one here, Christie said. The truck's empty.

Sorry, darl, I should have warned you, the pilot said. They had an outbreak of the plague round here.

Right, Christie said, but she wasn't really listening.

I stepped down into the heat. We'd only left Perth an hour ago, but already the city felt a world away. Six cows watched us from the end of the paddock. Beyond was the olive and gold of the bush, clicking and singing to itself.

I walked to the truck. There were keys in the ignition, and a note on the dashboard.

It's okay, I called. The surveyor got called into town. The truck's ours for the month. He's left directions.

From the airstrip we drove back up the valley through stands of fledgling karri gums. Fingers of light strummed across the truck. When we got to Enmore, Christie stepped down and looked to the scattering of empty houses, and the scrub and hills that rose beyond.

Christ, that's not a village, she said. There's not even a pub. Nothing.

There's the mine.

There's the collapsed mine.

We'll see. I nodded at the parched playing field beside the road. What about cricket?

She turned and her smile was brilliant. There's no one else to play with, mister. It's perfect. We've got nothing else to do.

For a whole month.

Better get started, then. The book says now's the best time.

. I came round to her side of the truck and kissed her. She looked up at me and I placed my hand on her stomach, then eased it down between her thighs. Her eyes half closed.

Sometimes these things make me feel young. Sometimes they make me feel like a dirty old man.


It was sunset when we pulled into the steep driveway. The company had rented us the house, a bungalow fronted by huge windows overlooking an arc of scrubby hills. There wasn't a neighbour in sight.

I killed the engine, and the playful squabble of parrots sounded in the trees above. Someone had built a rough rock cairn atop the slope to the west. Christie stepped from the truck and climbed towards it. She stopped abruptly.

Oh, Christ. Look at this.

I clambered after her and drew up short. The ground cleaved open before us, dropping sharply into the cut of the mine. Bands of silver greys and ochre stains ran down towards the floor. The bottom lay deep in shadow, but I could make out the debris from the collapse.

My god, I said. I didn't know the house would be so close.

Christie looked from the mine back to the clearing

that held our new home. Show me your arm, she said. Show me that scar again.

I turned my arm to the day's last light. She placed her finger over the first puncture mark below the line of the scar.

It's a map, she said. This one's us.


## 2


At seven on Monday I pulled myself away from Christie's gentle breathing. I scoured the tang of sex from my skin, shaved and walked to meet the surveyor at the mouth of the mine. A faint mist trapped the sun between the trees. I was pleased to hear my boots upon the road, and to see parrots launch their bodies through the air, and to know that Christie, lying warm inside the house, might already be pregnant. I'd spent my youth in fear of procreation. I could barely comprehend this new pleasure, to hold her close and shut my eyes and let life flow unhindered. I wore my shirt half unbuttoned under my high-vis vest and did not care if I looked foolish.

I reached the road at the bottom of the gully and then the mouth of the open-cut mine. One side remained sheer. The other had collapsed utterly, its viscera spilled onto the floor. Among rocks the size of cars, mature trees reached for the light. I stood and studied the mess.

Just on eight the surveyor pulled up. He was very young. He had a clean-shaven, undercooked face and an ambitious handshake that made me embarrassed for him.

Morning, I said. I'm Steven.

Pete. Sorry about Saturday—I got called away. You guys settle in all right?

I nodded. Thanks. Great place. I hadn't realised we'd be so close.

Yeah, the only houses round here are on mining land.

We saw the clearings from the plane. Neighbours?

Nah, Pete said. Ruins mostly. They were all bought from the mine by the one family but they're gone now. Not much missed, either.

So it's just us?

Yeah. The cave-in finished the town. Everyone left for Kal.

And that was—?

Nineteen sixteen. Have a look at this.

Pete returned to his ute and fetched an old black-and-white photo of the mine before the collapse. The cut was narrow and twice as deep as now, its dark expanse latticed with props fashioned from whole trees. A crew of serious-faced men looked from their century into ours.

Lot of men working that, I said.

It was a miracle no one was hurt. Happened on a Sunday. All the old machinery's still down there.

And you live locally?

Market Road. Family's been here forever. My grand-parents still talk about getting this place reopened.

Well, it doesn't look—I said, but then I saw the expression on Pete's face. It doesn't look easy, but we've got a month to figure it out.

Pete nodded slowly. So, is that your daughter you've come with?

I stared at the man, but there was no malice in his eyes. If anything, a trace of bovine hope. I felt embarrassed again, and that made me spiteful.

Yes, I said. My daughter.

Nice. Family time?

Family time. Let's get started.


When I got back to the house that afternoon there were six .22 calibre bullets of faded brass strewn across the kitchen table. Someone had cut the tips off with a hacksaw.

Christie, I called. Christie?

The sliding door to the bathroom rolled open. Christie was wearing running shoes and shorts, and an old T-shirt of mine she'd shrunk in the wash, the week she moved into my place in Mandera. Her face was glowing. Hi, she said.

Where did these come from?

I found them in an old ute. Why are they like that?

Do more damage. Where's the ute?

You want to go for a walk?

We strolled down to the road among slender saplings the colour of ash. Blackberry sprawled from the ditches. The track went past our lone letterbox and climbed the other side.

Christie held my hand. How'd you go today? she said.

Not too bad. Pete's a nice-enough bloke. It doesn't look good for the mine, though. The lateral subsistence is much worse than they made out.

What'd Pete say?

I shrugged. The locals are all keen to make it work… You know, he asked if you were my daughter.

Christie groaned. What'd you tell him?

I said you were.

Christie pulled her hand away and rabbit-punched me in the shoulder. You're kidding, right? She looked me in the eye. Steven! What the hell for?

I don't know. Avoiding small-town gossip? I'm more than twice your age.

That's not avoiding gossip! What if he saw us kissing on the road?

What if he saw me do this?

Stop it, she said. Stop it.

Through the trees I caught a glimpse of white. We broke from the track and stepped over a collapsing fence of hand-cut posts. The ute sat ringed by slag heaps and the telltale humps of open shafts.

There, Christie said. The bullets were in the glove box.

The ute had no plates and the ignition had been hotwired. A scribbled nest of leaves and string lay on the driver's seat. The bonnet was up, and someone had prised the serial plate from the engine block. I looked around at the destroyed landscape and the rusted car and Christie standing with my T-shirt fitted tight across her breasts. I pressed myself to her.

All those bullets, I said. Great place to make a mess.

You know, old man, you don't perform and I'll throw you down a mineshaft.

I laughed, and tried to sit Christie on the tailgate of the ute. It was just the right height.

Quit it, she said. You have to tell Pete I'm not your daughter.

I nodded, caressing the back of her neck. Of course. I'll tell him first thing.

You better. What do you think happened here?

No idea.

Do you think this is one of the clearings? The ones we saw from the air?

I stepped back and looked reluctantly down the hill. Yes, I said. I rolled up my sleeve and looked at the scar. The second one. Here.

That's so weird, Christie said. I wonder what it means?

Who cares? Right now I have to get you home.

## 3

The next day we rose early to go for a walk before I started work. Christie wanted to find the third clearing. The day's first light brushed the tops of the gums with gold. In a terracotta birdbath beside the front path a pair of nimble honeyeaters splashed and flapped and then were gone among the leaves.

I like it here, I said. You don't get that in Mandera.

I guess, Christie said.

What do you mean, you guess?

It's so quiet. Especially when you're away at work. It's a bit freaky.

A bit freaky? You'll get used to it.

Sometimes I speak to Christie as if she were a school girl.

We followed the same track as the day before. Old rain had washed deep channels through the dirt, and here and there spines of rock surfaced from the deep. I pointed them out to Christie.

Basalt, I said. Six million years old. Granite. Three billion years.

If we have a boy, Christie said, let's call him Granite.

Do you think you might already be pregnant? I couldn't stop myself asking.

Jeez! she said, laughing. Is it that urgent?

I thought of the need to procreate that had seized my

friends over the decades. The women first, then the men, maddened by the desire to breed. In my work, time was measured in millions of years. Against that slow patience of stone the need to reproduce had always seemed like vanity. Then I met Christie, and I felt my slackened skin beneath her hand, and I saw that the real vanity was my own. I had not thought to have children because I had not thought that I would die.

We reached a saddle and began to descend. Down in the trees I saw the pale silver eye of a tin roof. A small house of tawny stone lay in the third clearing, bordered by marshy ground ripe with the prints of roos. The house had empty sockets in place of doors and windows. Its garden had long ago drowned in a sea of gorse.

Hello, Christie called softly. Anyone home?

We stood and listened, and there was no sound. Christie walked ahead and entered the house, calling as she went. I followed her onto a rough dirt floor and let my eyes adjust. A stack of timber stood against one wall, keeping watch over a mouse-soiled mattress. I wondered idly who had used that bed.

At the back I found a tiny bedroom, with a mezzanine built into the far wall. Above the platform a stained-glass window glowed ochre and gold in the early sun.

Look at this, I called.

Christie came up behind me and put her arms around my waist.

It's the only thing they finished, she said wistfully. It's beautiful. Maybe we could finish the rest for them.

It wouldn't take much, I said. It's quiet, though. Not too freaky for you?

No. I wonder why they never finished it?

Because they were hippies.

Steven.

Because things happen, I said. People make plans that don't work out.

Christie was quiet. Then she said, Do you think this will work out?

What, this house?

No, this. She took my hand and placed it on her belly.

I thought of all the plans I had made and dropped before Christie was even born. I thought of her plans to finish her degree and travel, and how readily I had accepted their abandonment. I thought of my mother, meeting Christie for the first time: how she'd held her knife and fork like she didn't know what they were for, and how her face was confused and brave and shamed, and how her shame at times became my own. I thought of my father's joking that he wanted me to father a grand-child, not marry one. My friends who would not meet my eye, and those too keen to meet Christie's. Her own family, somewhere up in the Pilbara, unmet, unknown, never discussed; just the freight of their history within her youthful frame.

We had only known each other a year. The pull of that year had been strong. But to the stones of this house and the shoals of rock that ran beneath, the pull of that year meant nothing.

Will it work out?

Why not, I said. Then, more forcefully, Yes.

## 4

Christie woke me on Saturday with coffee and a week-old newspaper saved from Perth. The sun was long up. We sat in its heat with our shirts off. I looked to the sweet curved shadows below Christie's breasts, and soon was kneeling by her side to lick at her nipples. I tasted the sharp scent of coffee on my breath and her morning warmth, and felt her hand in my hair.

There was a sudden crunching of tyres over gravel. Pete's ute powered up the drive, a flash of green. The weight of Christie's breast was at my lips and then was gone. She dashed into the house and I lurched to my feet, fumbling for my shirt, working at buttons.

Morning, Steve.

Pete's voice was breezy. Out of his work clothes he looked even younger. He'd spiked his hair, and I caught a whiff of something perfumed and chemical.

I was in the area, he said. Brought you guys some rabbits.

Thanks, I said. Come in. Coffee?

Pete put his bundle on the kitchen table. With my back to him I refilled the percolator and set it on the stove. I tried to be calm.

Jeez, he said. What are they for?

I turned. Pete was inspecting the hacksawed nose of one of the bullets.

That'd make a scene, he said. Roo shooting?

No, we just found them.

Pete looked at me, quizzical. The hallway door opened and Christie came in. She'd changed into a long-sleeved top and jeans, despite the heat. Her cheeks were flushed. She looked irritable and gorgeous.

Pete stood up too quickly. Hi, he said. I'm Pete.

Christie.

They shook hands, and I saw that they were about the same age.

So, how you like it out here? Pete's voice was full of warmth.

Not bad, Christie said. She looked at the bag of meat on the table and I could see her clocking why he'd come. I smiled to myself. Smart girl.

You got uni holidays? Pete asked.

No. I'm not studying at the moment.

Yeah, cool. Pete leaned forward, waiting for her to say more, and I had the absurd feeling that I was intruding. I pretended to look for something in the walk-in pantry.

So you look more like your mum, hey? I heard Pete say. I just mean, 'cause with your skin you don't look so much like—

I went back out into the kitchen clutching a bag of sugar. Pete tailed off. The coffee pot began to murmur on the stove.

So, what's to do round here on a Saturday? I asked.

Pete gave a half shrug. Go into town, he said. Do your shopping, go down the pub for dinner. Actually, there's a party at Jono's tonight. You guys should come for a beer.

Thanks, I said. But I think we're planning a quiet one tonight. It's been a long week.

I don't know, Christie said, her brown eyes daring me. I haven't been to a party in ages.

You should totally come, Pete said.

I'll see if I can convince him, Christie said. He's got your number?

Yeah. Or I could…pick you up?

Christie smiled. I'll let you know. Steve, I'm going for a walk.

The pot was boiling now. I turned off the element. You don't want any coffee?

No.

Okay. I'll come find you. Where?

Other side of the mine. You've got the map.

I'd be careful, Pete said. There's a lot of unmarked

shafts round here. Stick to the tracks.

Yes, Dad, Christie said in a mocking, flirtatious voice.


With Christie gone, Pete didn't stick around. I saw him off and started the climb up behind the house. A few hundred metres along I found the head of the mine. I stood and looked out over the vast bite it took from the valley. I was certain Pete hadn't seen us, but I felt unsettled. I wasn't sure which was more strange: pretending Christie was my daughter, or the fact that she wasn't.

Down the other side of the slope I found a crumbling dry-stone wall. The surrounding bush was peppered with the alien green of European trees. I felt a small thrill of discovery.

Christie? I called.

Steven!

The air smelled different here, snatches of something foreign and sweet. I moved clear of the bush and found the crumbling stone footings of an old stamper battery. There were still a few of these things running when I was young: the hammer of engines, the earth pulverised beneath iron hoofs. The main building here was gone to a scattering of stone but beyond, more recent outbuildings sagged beneath the weight of creepers.

In here, Christie called. Look.

I moved towards the nearest shed. Christie emerged from the darkness. She placed something small and heavy in my palm. It was another .22 shell, this time with its nose intact.

You haven't told Pete yet, she said.

I pursed my lips. No. Sorry. I haven't been able to find the right—

Don't be weird about it, she said. Tell him, okay?

I will.

Christie looked down at the bullet. What do you think of that?

Coincidence, I said. They're pretty common.

Boring. Maybe the guy who lived here dumped that ute after a robbery.

What? Someone lived here?

Yeah. And just abandoned the place. Come and look.

The shed had been roughly lined with fibro panels to create two small rooms. Creepers had prised apart the boards, and daylight gleamed like jewels above. In the living room an armchair faced a window looking over the valley. A side table held dusty photographs: a middle-aged couple tiny against the red stone bulk of Uluru; the man in rubber waders proudly holding a fish; the man again, arm around what looked like his daughter. She was a striking, sharp-featured girl in school uniform and knee-high socks. I crouched beside a swollen chipboard bookcase and fingered the contents. Nabokov. *The I Ching*. Books I had read.

Educated people, I said.

There was a camp stove on a bench in the corner.

Christie held up a rusty tin of soup. Doesn't look like he ever learned how to cook.

You don't know it was a he.

Look at the bath! she said, sounding delighted. Only a man could let it get that disgusting.

Outside the back door a tiny bathtub crouched beneath an old-fashioned showerhead. It was full of flaking paint and leaves, and was darkly scummed with grease.

And look in the bedroom, Christie said. Men's clothes. He didn't even take them all.

In the bedroom a row of dusty shirts lay on the still-made bed. A pair of men's leather shoes peeked out from under the bed. There was something about those shoes I could not bear.

I have to go outside, I said.

And this, Christie said, triumphant. This is his treasure. Look.

She placed a stack of old VHS boxes in my hand. I turned them to the light. Beneath a layer of dirt I saw pink flesh and open mouths. *Girl on Girl. Screamers. Young and Fuckable.*

Oh.

They've still got tapes in them. Creepy!

I opened *Young and Fuckable*. There was an unmarked home-recording VHS tape inside. I closed it and handed the tapes back.

I have to go outside, I said again.

## 5

We left the shack and I walked on ahead by myself. I needed the open air of the bush. I passed down the slope and began to breathe, but the trees thinned and I came immediately to another clearing. In the centre, with a commanding view of the plains to the west, was a house-sized mound of charred debris. I felt sick. A skeletal chimney rose from a rubble of half-burned books and timbers gagged with weeds.

I shaded my eyes from the noontime glare and saw it all. The man drunk in bed with his guilty pleasure burning quickly down. His hand wavering with sleep, the glowing tip sighing into polyester sheets. Suffocated into waking. The dead terror of pulling yourself hand over hand down your own greasy hallway, birthed out the front steps into the night while at your back your life was quickly and mercilessly used up. The terrible heat on your face. The smoke in your scorched lungs. The loneliness to follow. *Screamers. Young and Fuckable.*

Christie walked among the ruins.

The poor guy, I said. Pete told me about him. He burned the place down smoking in bed.

What a stupid old fuck, Christie said.

I rounded on her. You know what, I said. I think Pete fancies you.

Christie flushed. What? So? He thinks I'm your daughter.

85

Shall I tell him you're not?

What are you going to say? You know how I was sucking my daughter's tits—well, that's not my daughter?

He didn't see anything. I'll tell him on Monday you're not available. He'll be disappointed. I reckon you're the only thing young and fuckable this side of Perth.

Fuck you, Christie said. That's not funny.

No, fuck you.

What's the matter with you? She sounded close to tears.

I stared at her, standing among the ruins in knee-high grass with her lips askew and her hair a dark tangle, and I was damn near overcome with the force of my need. I felt rage in me, rage and hunger, incoherent, geological. I had a vision of a girl flung back in the grass with her jeans around her ankles and someone, some weathered old man, me, straining away on top. I dropped my gaze.

It's this place, I said. It's getting to us.

Christie said nothing.

I need a break. Can we go into town? Have a meal at the pub?

She nodded warily. Okay.

## 6

In the truck on the way in, Christie broke the long silence.

Maybe it's the mine, she said.

What is?

Why everything feels so weird. Like the mine has some kind of—negative energy.

I don't know about negative energy, I said.

You're the one who said the place was getting to you. She paused. Maybe the mine's like a scar. Or a wound that hasn't healed. What if something bad happened there in the past?

I don't know. I doubt it.

But what about those bullets, and the ute and that burned house?

I shrugged. It's the past. It can't affect us.

Christie turned her head away and was quiet. Dusk was settling over the bush and I switched on the headlights. When I looked over again, I thought she had fallen asleep. Then I saw her watching my reflection in the glass.

Steven, she said.

Yes?

If the past can't affect us, how can we affect the future?

I took one hand from the wheel and squeezed her thigh, and smiled. By having children, I said.

As the light faded into evening we came past the stockyards and into the town. There was a wide street of neat shops with a handsome stone pub at the corner. Four-wheel-drives and utes filled the car park.

We sat for a moment with the engine ticking in the stillness.

Let's get one thing straight, Christie said. I'm not your daughter.

You're not my daughter, I said. I'm sorry I said that. That was stupid.

Yes, she said. She leaned over and kissed my cheek. Stupid. You need to tell people the truth. And I think you owe me a drink.

We pushed open the door of the pub. There were nods and a polite smile or two from the locals. I followed Christie to the bar, and tried not to stare at her switch-hipped walk.

What can I get you?

The woman behind the bar was about my age. She had grey hair pulled back from a tanned, no-nonsense face.

Crownie for him, Christie said. Have you got cider? Cider?

Sorry, Christie said. I just—

Course we got cider. I'm kidding. Apple or pear?

Pear, thanks.

The woman looked at me with interest. You're the engineer come to look at the mine, right?

Yes. I'm Steven. This is Christie.

Lindy. How's it going out there?

So far, so good.

It'd be bloody marvellous if you got it running again. There you go. She placed our drinks on the bar and tucked a stray hair behind her ear. She smiled at me. So, how you liking Enmore? Not too lonely?

Well—

Yeah, Christie cut in. A bit. It's pretty quiet.

Not much to do out there at your age, the woman said. How you keeping busy?

Christie shrugged. Reading books. Or going exploring. It's a weird place.

Oh yeah? the woman said lightly.

There's a stolen ute dumped behind our house. I found bullets in the glove box.

The woman raised her eyebrows.

It's been there a while, I said. But I guess we could report it.

Wouldn't bother, she replied. There's cars dumped all over round here.

And, Christie said, there's a place that burned down that's got a really creepy vibe.

Oh. I know the one.

You knew those people? What happened?

It's okay, I said. It's none of our—

Bloke was an alcoholic, the woman said. She took a cloth and began wiping down the bar. House burned down, wife left him, daughter ran away. It happens.

Definitely weird, Christie said. She sipped her drink. You know the other thing? Steven's got this scar that's like a map of the mine and all those houses.

A map?

Check it out.

Christie lifted my arm into the light, and I could see the woman watching, her top lip faintly curled. I pulled my arm away, uncomfortable, embarrassed.

It's like the mine's a scar itself, Christie said. I reckon something bad happened out there.

Yeah, like what? The woman threw her cloth into the sink, and there was a note in her voice I did not like.

Something full on, Christie said. Not sure I want to know.

Anyway, I said, let's—

Maybe, the woman said, lowering her voice, you'll find bodies at the bottom of the mine.

Christie leaned forward, nodding.

People killed in the cave-in. Or maybe the mine was on an Aboriginal burial ground. But you know what I really think?

What?

I think they threw bodies in there after a massacre.

Oh, shit, Christie said, and there was a change in her face: youthful fascination pinched out by something hard and cold. You think so?

Oh, for sure, the woman said, her voice now ripe with scorn. There were massacres all round here. Got to be connected. Your Abos, the scar, the mine, the ute, the burned house, yeah, and the man who messes with his daughter. *Got* to be connected.

Christie said nothing, her face slammed shut. I lifted

the cold glass of my bottle to my lips but could not drink. I felt old and wrong.

Or, the woman said, it's just a bunch of poor fucks living in the middle of nowhere, with no jobs. There's no mystery. Bad shit happens to people like that all the time. You get that mine opened and watch it get better. Seventeen.

Excuse me? I said.

Seventeen dollars. Round here you have to pay for your drinks.

I took out my wallet and handed her a twenty.

She walked to the till, then called back over her shoulder. It's just a hole in the fucking ground. Your daughter's been reading too many books.

I could feel fury shimmering off Christie like heat from the Pilbara at noon. I found her hand.

She's not my daughter, I called back.

Two men along the bar turned to look, and I saw their gaze slide from me to Christie.

We're partners, I said, as loudly as I dared.

# THE LOTUS EATERS

*On the tenth day we reached the land of the Lotus-eater,*
*who live on a food that comes from a kind of flower...*
*I sent two of my company to see what manner of men*
*the people of the place might be, and they had a third*
*man under them. They started at once, and went about*
*among the Lotus-eaters, who did them no hurt, but*
*gave them to eat of the lotus, which was so delicious that*
*those who ate of it left off caring about home.*
            —Homer, THE ODYSSEY

IT WAS tourist season when I arrived. Resorts gleamed among the jungle. Backpackers filled the bars. I crossed the steel bridge at Nong Khiaw in suffocating heat. The locals lay sleeping in the shade. Ahead on the road I heard a mocking singsong voice cry out in French.

I am so *layyyy-zeee!*

In a roadside clearing, four of my compatriots sat slumped beside a bamboo shack. They wore the red-eyed smirks of the drunk-for-weeks. Empty bottles covered the table in front of them.

The man who had spoken was handsome and skel-etal. Against the deep tough brown of his skin, his singlet was shockingly white. He threw up his hands. Every day I say *Enough! I'm going!* But every day they get me. They say *Laos-laos!* I drink and the day is gone. So I say *Tomorrow! Tomorrow, I'll go.* But every day's the same. I am so *layyyy-zeee!*

The man sounded delighted. He pronounced the word like he was diving into a deep azure pool.

Friends, I called. Room for one more?

They looked up at my approach. A woman rose imme-diately. She seemed relieved.

Take my place, she said. It's time for me to go.

She kissed them each in turn and said goodbye and went on up the road. I dropped my pack and took her seat.

Back in Paris I was a musician, said the man in the white singlet. I love music! But there was no rest. Life was work, work, work. A beautiful thing became a curse, and so I ran away. Here there is only one thing to do: nothing.

His hand went among the slum of bottles, toppling them in search of drink. He poured a thick clear spirit into dirty glasses, and set one before each of us.

*Laos-laos*, he said. Rice whisky, aged in a bucket. France makes the wine of the gods. Laos makes the liquor of ghosts. To laziness!

To laziness, a lithe pale woman said. To laziness and idleness and cant.

We threw it down, and I felt it crawl back up my spine.

I'm Louis, the man said. This is Céline. She's a lawyer. She was a partner in Casteaux et fils, no less. But of course, she prefers *ooooo-pium*!

The woman turned to me. She had an exquisite, intelligent face cratered with orange-red sores: no doubt some obscure tropical disease, expensive to catch. I thought I would like to sleep with her.

The more I learned of the law? she said, and gave the barest amused shrug, as if the air itself was too heavy.

And this is Maxime, Louis said. He's a chef. He drinks like a chef. But he hates to cook!

The man had a heavy beard, and the kind of morose gravity that makes talkative people act like fools. Filling his silence would be like shovelling sand into the sea. He laid a possessive paw across Céline's shoulders, and tilted his head at me. *Salut.*

We drank a hole in the afternoon, and I saw that we would be friends. They were armchair nihilists, obsessed with escape and, once escaped, obsessed with looking back.

Why did you leave France? Louis said. Please, it's our favourite game.

You want to know the truth? I said.

Tell us, Louis said. Why?

Because the world is ending.

Oh-ho, Louis cried. Now I know we will be friends! But why will it end?

Because the planet will throw us off, I said. The polar caps are going, the glaciers are going. Soon it'll tip. Heatwaves and droughts and floods. Soon we'll be living in hell.

Oh-ho, Louis repeated. You are one of them. You really believe that?

No, I said. It is unfashionable to believe anything at all. But I act as if it's true.

How? Céline asked. How do you act?

I opt out. I refuse to participate.

Of course, Céline said. You save the world by flying around the world getting drunk.

Why shouldn't he, Louis said. Drink has been saving the world for centuries. Luang! Come!

A face appeared in the window of the shack: a middle-aged man, his face crushed and fragrant with sleep.

Luang, Louis said, the world is ending again. Get us four *laap*. Another bottle of *laos-laos*. Make it quick.

The man came round to clear our table, dreamlike in the heat's embrace.

What is your name? I murmured to him.

His name is Luang, Louis said. Those are his children.

Beside us in the road, three barefoot children played a fast-forward game of pétanque, lobbing silver balls into the ripening twilight.

One dollar, two dollar, three dollar, four, Louis said. He's saving our money to send his children to university.

96

He thinks it will make their lives better.

Luang smiled; he seemed embarrassed.

He is a good man, Louis said. But slow, like his country. Few things happen at very low speed. Nothing will change.

That's why I love it here, Céline said. Every day is the same as the last.

How long have you been here? I asked her.

Céline's eyes were milky grey, an empty mirror for the fading sky. A long time, she said.

I smiled. How long?

One hundred and twenty years.

My smile wavered. She lit a cigarette, and rested her chin in her hand. A thin drift of smoke curled between us.

This bar has been full of drunken Frenchmen, she said, since the year eighteen ninety-three. It has never been empty. These seats pass like batons in a relay. We sit and try to remember why we are here, but the truth is—we have come here to forget.

To forget what? I asked.

Again that shrug, shaking off the weight of the air.

That is a good question, she said.


It was burning season when I arrived. Fires gleamed among the jungle. Smoke filled the valleys. I crossed the iron bridge at Nong Khiaw. The old river below was restless, and the new road above freighted with a secret traffic pushing south. Planes droned overhead. There were rumours that the borders would close. Ahead on the road I heard a rough sardonic voice cry out in French.

I am so *layyyy-zeee*!

There was a bamboo shack in a clearing cut from the jungle. Two men and a woman sat slumped under a Coca-Cola awning.

Of course we should flee! the man was saying. He lolled in his chair, wild with false mirth. But why? I tell you this because you are too drunk to remember: we put them up to it, so we should answer for it. We paid them, armed them, put fire in their blood. They pulled the trigger, but the deeds are ours—

He broke off to watch my approach. His sideburns were unkempt, his fedora pushed back rakishly on his head.

Mademoiselle, he called. You are French, no?

Yes.

Do you hate your country?

I shrugged. Of course.

Good! Luang! Another chair.

Have mine, the Frenchwoman said. What the hell—there may still be time.

She kissed the two men, picked up a small valise and went quickly up the road. I laid my bag in the dirt and took her seat.

I am Louis, the man said. You are?

Céline, I said.

This is Maxime, Louis said. He is a soldier. He drinks like a soldier but he hates to fight.

The man sat closed behind a heavy beard. He was perhaps Moroccan, and he had a damaged silence about him, like artillery stilled at dusk. He looked at me and said nothing.

It is lucky you hate your country, Louis said, because you can never go back. The evacuation planes have flown. They are closing the borders. I for one think we must celebrate.

His hand went among the arsenal of bottles. He seized each one and, finding it empty, hurled it into the trees. He found one that was full and poured three cups.

*Laos-laos*, Louis said. Rice whisky. If you have any nerve left at all, this will dissolve it. To despair!

To despair!

I threw it down, and my nerves lit up like jungle canopy under napalm.

You know the Pathet Laos have quit their caves? Louis said. They are moving on the capital.

Do you think they will succeed? I asked.

The Vietcong did, Maxime said. And the Khmer Rouge. Why not the Pathet Laos?

Why not? Louis cried. Because everyone is so *layyyy-zeee*! It will take them a thousand years to reach the capital.

We will drink ourselves to death first!

He swung to me, and I felt his gaze linger over the sores on my face.

Céline, he said, why did you not return to France while you had the chance?

Return to France? I said. I have just escaped.

Bravo! Louis said. He refilled my glass. Tell me why you escaped.

Because it is the end of the world.

Of course it is, he said. The question is still why?

I gave the barest shrug. Imperialism? Bourgeois conservatism? Sexism?

Oh-ho, Louis said. You are one of them. What of liberalism and feminism and socialism? Are these not the ends of the world?

I wish they were, I said. But sixty-eight has taken a job and a mortgage.

Oh-ho, he repeated. You are disappointed in your revolution, and so you run away.

There is a real revolution here, I said. I raised my glass into the low burning sun. If communism is the end of the world, let us witness it.

We shall drink to that. Luang! Come!

A face rose in the window of the shack: a moon at the sickle turn, sharp with fear.

Luang, the world is ending again, Louis cried. He snapped his fingers. Another bottle of *laos-laos*. Quickly.

The man moved among us with a bottle of the thick clear spirit.

Thank you, I murmured to him. What is your name?

His name is Luang, Louis said. Those are his children.

Beside us in the road three barefoot children played at being soldiers. They pointed their sticks; they fell and jerked in the dust.

Luang is Pathet Laos, Louis said. I know that, and he knows that I know.

Luang smiled, yet he seemed afraid.

He is a good man, Louis said. He sides with the communists because he believes life will be better for his children. But nothing changes. This country has no history.

Out on the road the children scattered. A young soldier in ill-fitting fatigues passed on a motorbike. He turned at the bridge and came back. He looked us over with curiosity and disgust, and spoke in Laotian. A change came over Louis. He replied sharply to the soldier and they both began to laugh.

There is a company of Pathet Laos guerrillas coming west, Louis said. They are looking for a man they claim is helping the royalists. I told him I am the man they seek but, like all Frenchmen, I am too lazy to flee. He thinks I am very funny.

Louis poured a shot of *laos-laos* for the soldier and they drank together. The soldier remounted his motorbike and continued across the bridge. We sat in silence. Louis poured still more drinks, and I saw his hands were shaking.

Actually, I am not joking, he said. I am the man they seek. But how can I leave? I am too *layyyy-zeee*! Perhaps I will go tomorrow.

Tomorrow, Maxime said. I have been waiting for that a long time.

How long? I asked.

Eighty years, he said, and there was perhaps a hint of amusement about his face.


It was monsoon season when I arrived. The sky roared. Water filled the valleys. It lay in gleaming pools along the road and in the roadside ditches where I walked. I travelled at night and slept by day among the wide green pandanus. I swam the river at Muang Ngoi below the wooden bridge, stroking out into a flat grey dark. My fatigues clung like small wet hands. I scrambled up the bank and regained the cart track. I heard laughter ahead. A voice crying out in French.

But I am so *layyyy-zeee*!

There was a bar beside the track, and two bodies pressed together at an outside table. Their limbs surfaced like pale islands in the pre-dawn dark. Bottles gleamed upon the ground. I heard the river's restless murmur and the whispered laughter on their breath.

Come here, said a woman's voice. Oh, you must. Darling.

A spill of curls. The svelte curve of her legs around a man's naked back.

I cannot.

You must.

I cannot. I am too *layyyy-zeee*!

You are too drunk!

I am sorry. I have tried, but it is impossible—to be too drunk.

They broke apart to the musical clatter of bottles.

Hello? the man called. Who's there?

The woman laughed. Surely it is my father. Come to fetch me home and cut off your balls.

Welcome! the man called. Drink with us, Monsieur Casteaux. It will steady your hand for the cut.

The man lit a lantern, and wild shadows swung about the trees. By the light he was handsome and skeletal, without a shirt, his trousers agape. She was just as thin, her cheekbones sharp. She pulled down her skirt but did not care to hide her breasts.

I stepped forward and their laughter dimmed. I was dripping wet, unshaven and exhausted. The man said something in a language I did not know.

Room for another? I asked in French.

You are French? the man said.

Of course.

But you look—you look like you need a drink.

I must go, the woman said.

Stay, the man said. We are not finished.

*I* am not finished, the woman said, her face lit by mirth and drink. And you cannot finish me. I will see you later. I must get some sleep.

She hunted the shadows for her blouse. She buttoned it crookedly, then swayed off towards the bridge. I watched her depart from the lantern's fragile sphere. The man read my expression as concern.

Do not worry, he said. Mademoiselle Casteaux is unkillable. She will dance upon our graves. I'm Rochefort. Call me Louis. Drink this.

He handed me a tumbler of something poisonous. At the first sip my empty stomach screamed. I kept my face unmoved.

The natives make it, he said. It has the peculiar quality of making time stop. You are…French Foreign Legion, are you not?

This time I could not keep the surprise from my face. I had torn the insignia from my uniform but to no end. I was too exhausted to lie, or to run. I could only hope that such a man would not report me.

I was, I said.

You *were*? But you cannot leave the Legion.

I believe you can.

I could see him thinking, very slowly. You have

deserted? All the way from—Indochine? On *foot*?

I said nothing. He seemed delighted.

But you are perfectly mad! We must drink to this. And you must tell me why!

I threw back my head and drained my glass, and the horizon swung away beneath me. I felt my nerves fill with the cold, billowing fire of mustard gas.

Why desert? I said. Because the world is to end.

Oh-ho! he cried. Now I know we shall be friends. How will it end?

You have heard the news from Europe?

No. We are blessed to receive no news whatsoever.

They say Herr Hitler will march on Paris. They say it will be much worse than last time.

Oh, that, he said. Surely that is not serious.

I am afraid it is. I fought in the first war and survived. I will not survive a second.

Bravo. And they are conscripting again?

As we speak.

Louis began to laugh, long and hard, until he was close to retching. His sunken face seemed fashioned wholly out of sweat.

Forgive me, he said at last. It is too perfect. I have been in Laos a long time. I avoided the first war and now it seems I have managed to avoid a second. Come, let us get you breakfast. Luang!

No one answered. There was a rough shack behind us,

swallowed by the jungle palms. Louis rose and opened the door and entered the darkness. He emerged half dragging a man, and I glimpsed a face chaotic with surprise and sleep. Louis pushed him down against the wall.

Wake up, for god's sake, Louis said. The world is ending again. Get us two *laap* and a pipe of poppy. And give me your shirt.

The man looked up at him uncertainly. Louis spoke sharply in Laotian. The man unbuttoned.

Here, Louis said to me. Put this on. And give him yours. It will be our little joke.

I began to suspect that the Frenchman was a fool. But I was not going to refuse a shirt. To be caught in my own uniform was to be shot. I unbuttoned and handed my shirt to the native.

Here, I murmured, trying to apologise with my eyes. What is your name?

His name is Luang, Louis said. Those are his children.

I had not noticed the two small figures curled beside the shack. They were awake, dark eyes watching their father.

He agitates in secret for decolonisation, Louis said. I know that. He knows that. And now he wears the uniform of those who would die for France!

Luang looked away. He seemed upset.

He is a good man, Louis said. He is only treasonous because he imagines life will be better for his children without us. But of course there will be no mutiny. There is no history here. Nothing changes.

But I have come, I said.

Certainly, Louis said. And there was one before you, and there will be one after.

But you, I said. Who was here before you?

He smiled at that, his thin moist lips stretched across stained teeth. Before me?


I arrived in an alien season, neither summer nor autumn nor winter nor spring. The sky was a tumescent weight. The afternoons swelled but did not burst, and I felt my head would burst instead. I was glad, for there was not the meanest crevice left for thought.

We stepped from the barges at a place the natives knew as Nong Khiaw. We made a gloomy camp above that wide brown serpent where it twisted south. Someone had been here before us: the ruin of a sad thatched hut, and a table on cleared ground. I sat at this table and surveyed the land. High cliffs of limestone rose on three sides, and the verdant jungle tumbled down. It was a fine vantage. How strange to kick a cross in the dirt, and here would be a city!

All this I wrote in my dispatch. But my secret reason lay within the sombre darkness of the place, in the heat hanging thick upon us like damnation. For surely here was the end of the earth: the furthest one could get from the Eiffel Tower, that stiletto through the heart of the city I had loved. Paris seemed to me now some lost and insane dream, and my lover's face but a face glimpsed once in a crowded station. They told me white men cannot work in the tropics. They go mad in the heat. That is why they sent me here, and that is why I came. It is a neat justice when the punishment pleases both the guilty and the dead.

I ordered my possessions be unloaded from the boats. The coolies dragged them up, a chain of ants carrying off the artefacts of some junked civilisation. They dropped my velvet *chaise longue*, and as it cartwheeled and smashed apart upon the mud I laughed like a horse. One simply *must* own a *chaise longue* in Paris. Here, one must simply throw the bloated thing into a river.

By day's end I was drunk. I sat at that rough wooden table with my worldly goods, obedient and useless, arranged beneath chandeliers of jungle fruit. It seemed the walls of my house in *le seizième* had dissolved within the swarming dusk, and just the furniture remained. I toasted the mahogany dining table. I toasted the high-backed chairs. I toasted the profound emptiness of my feather bed.

Sir.

One of my soldiers stood before me; and behind him, a native with clinging child. The native seemed distressed.

Sir, the soldier said. We can find no nails among the supplies.

This is most dismaying, I said. The stew will be bland.

The man did not laugh. His face was not unkind, but distaste made it ugly. He knew why I had been sent here.

Sir, we have dispatched a boat, but it will be some weeks before a dwelling can be built. We fear for your furniture.

Let the furniture rot, I said. I have brandy to last two hundred years. Who is this man?

He would speak with you, sir. He says this is his house and table.

He lives here?

Sir. He was away when we arrived. He brings you a gift.

The native offered a clay flagon. I unstoppered it: sweet ghastly fumes, a mouthful of fire. Men crawling through paddies. Black tongues and stones for eyes. Flames.

What is this? I asked.

*Laos-laos.* A strong spirit.

And his name?

The soldier asked the man, and the man moved his mouth. To me it sounded like *Luang*, meaning town or place in the native tongue. It was as good a name as any.

Tell Luang he may work for me. I shall want more of his medicine. And bring me my pipe.

The soldiers lit the lamps and retired. The coolies sat off down beside the river, living in another century, and it was just myself and this fellow Luang. He stood in the doorway of the hut and watched me at his table. His mouth was a dark line. I dragged a leather armchair to the light.

Drink with me, I said.

Beneath the lamps, the man seemed older. Older and stranger, and yet I felt I could know him. There were lines raked about his eyes and down his cheeks as on my own. His black hair was drifting to a coarsened silver, and he perched uncertainly on the chair. We drank together, heads back, throats exposed. He watched me all the way down, like a bird with a snake.

Do you hate France? I asked.

He made no reply.

Of course you do not, I said. You cannot hate that which you do not know. You cannot even speak of it. But I can. I have come in the name of France, and I would erase France from the face of the earth. I would erase all countries and all nations. It is not the scandal. Scandal is not the end of the world. It is everything else. Everything that would make us scandalous.

I laughed at my own wit. I laughed, but the spectre of scandal had been raised, and now it must be drowned.

I took up my pipe, and turned the ivory in my hand. The piece was old, from a bazaar in Rangoon. I turned down the lamps and opened my pores, and I bent to the flame. I took the future into my lungs.

We are not here to forget what we have done, I said, letting the smoke curl between us, thin and lazy, a riddle too banal to solve. We are not fools. The past will not hurt us.

It is the future we must forget. We are here to escape what we will surely do.

From the river, the deranged stridency of frogs. Sweat ran and dripped from my brow in quickening rhythms. I drew down again upon the smoke, and I closed my eyes and it was suddenly there above us: the great wounded bird of progress. Steel talons reaching forth, its eyes put out, buckshot burning in its wings. The limestone crags were lit with fire, horizon to horizon, the clouds aflame. The jungle should burn and the cities should burn. I heard a mechanical screaming, felt iron and bone beneath my skin, saw her face, saw fields of corpses, cities of glass, cities of tents, rivers of ice, of people, faces, dreams, light, all—cancelled.

I lunged towards the native and the table tipped. The lanterns fell, blue fire breaking in waves across the ground. He leapt back from his chair, and I was in the dirt on my hands and knees.

The future must never reach us here, I cried out. Never. Surely you must understand.

Luang stood away at a distance, looking like one who has eaten meat that has turned. Then he came slowly forward, and crouched and peered into my face, and his eyes softened. I saw then that he had not understood. He had not understood at all.

# DATA FURNACE

I TAKE the London Overground to work—on foot. Snow crunches and squeaks beneath my boots. The last train to run this line's a rusted carcass, buried in a snowdrift at the bottom of the Surrey Quays cutting.

I work in IT. Before the Switch I was fat and timid, and I thought it was my fault. It's amazing how little of anything is your fault. Live in an era where you stumble out of bed and catch the train to work: you're fat. Live in an era where you stumble to work in knee-deep snow: no gym class can match that. I feel fit and decisive.

I leave the train line and cross the ice downriver of Tower Bridge. The wind-blasted shell of City Hall, the gutted apartments along the reach of the Thames, the abandoned spires of the City: they're all so deformed by frost

they look like they were designed by children. An evacuation plane struggles overhead. I choose not to watch. It
feels like every last breath of heat has been sucked from
the world.

Which is typical, really. The rest of the planet's on
its way to burning up, and we get an ice age. Thank you,
Britain, you miserable bastard.

From Wapping I detour west to wait for my workmate
Umi in the usual spot, beneath the memorial to the Great
Fire of London. I don't know how you'd commemorate the
desperate bonfire that's consuming the city today. When
the freeze slammed down it was firewood and coal first,
then the Regency tables and Ikea chairs, the carpets and
floorboards, staircases and doors, towels, TVs, PlayStations,
sex toys, tyres, dead animals, corpses—all burned.

I check my phone. Seven forty-eight. Umi's running
late, but then, she's not expecting me. I've been at the
airport for the best part of a month, waiting with my
family for an evac flight. I click the phone off and check
my reflection in the empty screen: a small, hopeful face
smudged behind thick glasses and beard. An old man's face,
Marie says, though I'm not yet forty. I blink, trying to
remember my speech.

Footsteps make me turn. At the edge of the square, a
tall figure in blazing red stands in the cold steel light.

George?

Umi! I yell.

She strides across the square, her energetic face full of worry. What happened to your flight?

Marie and Jordan made it out, I say. Last night.

What about you?

I meet Umi's gaze, and just like that my decisiveness flees. I look away.

Tell me you didn't put off leaving *again*, Umi says.

No, I mumble. I—missed the plane.

Oh, George! Umi says, with such exasperation that I realise this is the easiest lie. No one would believe me capable of more, or less.

They called the names and ten minutes later it was gone, I say. I was getting coffee.

Umi's hand goes to her mouth.

It wasn't even a very good coffee. The milk was burned.

George! Where are Marie and Jordan? Do you know who took them in?

I shake my head.

You should be at the airport. Find where they landed, get the next flight.

They said I had no chance. Miss a flight, back of the queue. It'll be months.

I know people at London City Airport. Let me make some calls.

The airports are all shutting down for winter, Umi. Maybe for good.

We'll find you the money for a private evac. It's not—

I'm bloody well staying! I shout.

I'm not sure which of us is more surprised. In the silence that follows, I hear someone singing, slow and childlike, in a neighbouring street.

Umi stares at me. You still don't want to leave, do you?

You don't, I say. You think we're going to be fine. You think humans can adapt. You've told me a thousand—

I'm not married, George.

I don't want to talk about it, I say. Let's go to work.

Umi stamps her feet in the cold. Your wife and son are gone, and you're coming in to work?

We're out of coffee at home.

Stop it.

Well, how else am I going to keep warm?

Umi looks up at the monument's frozen flame. Good question, she says.


Work is the Isle of Dogs Secure Data Centre. Umi and I are systems administrators. We've got four thousand servers locked in an old Victorian factory, hosting most of what's left of Britain's internet. The building's a jumble of towers, silos and gantries, built like an industrial cathedral, so heavy and sheer it could have been carved from solid brick. A flaking billboard takes up half the back wall. The slogan's gone, but you can still make out a woman's giant face. She looks like Margaret Thatcher, only hot, and encased in ice.

Inside the front door, I lean my baseball bat in the corner and brush snow from my beard. It's been a month but nothing's changed. Old Man Canary's already awake. He's a cheerful old homeless guy the boss lets live in the stairwell. His rheumy eyes peer out at us from his nest of green sleeping bags.

Back? he says, giving me a gummy grin.

I missed you too much, I say.

Here you go, friend, Umi says.

Today she's brought him two bread rolls. He pops one under each armpit to thaw. She films him on her phone.

Yes! he chortles. Winning!

Umi uploads the clip on our way up the stairs. The heat-stroked outside world is obsessed with videos of the stupid shit people do here to keep warm. My favourite's a group of teenagers driving a herd of cows up the stairs to their Hyde Park penthouse squat.

I'm smiling when we reach the disguised security door on the top floor, but straight away I get the feeling something's wrong. Umi's stopped talking, and I realise it's dangerously quiet. She opens the rusted fuse box on the wall and presses her thumb to the scanner. The door hisses open.

After the derelict stairwell it's like walking into a spaceship: long, gleaming aisles of black servers stacked ten high in glass-fronted cabinets. Bundles of cable branch overhead like arteries. Dotted among the servers are the towering remnants of the original factory machinery, all soot-iron black and thick with rust. High windows throw a glacial light across the ancient engines, pistons and gears. Everything stands dormant, like the frozen carcasses of long extinct species. Without the heat from the server exhaust fans it's unbelievably cold.

On the far side of the room Joe, the old French guy who owns the place, is sitting on the edge of his desk. He knocks snow from his woollen cap onto the floor. He looks round and his smile drops away.

George! he barks. You put off going *again*?

I missed my flight, I say, crossing the floor. What's going on?

*Your* flight? Joe says. What about Marie, and—

Gone, I say. Safe. Given a knighthood.

But—

Why's everything off?

Joe stares at me, and shakes his head. It's time for me to go too, he says.

I feel like I've been winded.

You see this? Joe says, and for the first time I notice his swollen face. I got jumped in Greenwich. They shot my outrider and I was lucky to get away. I can't wait for winter either; I'm not getting any younger. I hate to shut this place down, but I have to go.

I don't know what to say. I look over at Umi. Normally she's so full of ideas that there's no point in bothering with your own. Now she just shrugs. I give her a look like, what the hell—you knew about this?

What are we supposed to do? I say to Joe.

I waited till you were meant to be gone, he says. Go back to the airport.

You can't leave.

Joe raises his frosty eyebrows.

It can't last, I say. It switched, so it has to switch back. It's not so bad.

Joe crosses to the fire door. He shoots back the bolts and swings it open. Sunlight slices across the vast confusion of snow-collapsed roofs. In the distance, the toppled London Eye looks more like an ear.

Not so bad? he says.

Could be worse.

Joe laughs. It *will* be worse, and you're too scared to move. Did you ever hear about how to boil a frog?

How to *what*?

Boil a frog. You take a frog, and put him in a pot of boiling water, and he jumps right out. But you put him in cold water and turn up the heat, nice and slow? He stays until he is cooked.

The old geezer's lost his mind.

He gestures to the fire escape. I've put it off long enough, he says. Sometimes you just know when it's time to jump.

What, out the fire escape?

A metaphor, George. I'm going to Laos.

When? I ask.

Joe checks the time on his phone. Soon.

*Today?*

Umi's already shut most of this down. We weld the doors shut, and if things get better like you say, we'll come back.

You're just abandoning all this?

Joe looks pained. What can I do? We've abandoned the whole country. I lock up, and I hope.

I want to argue, but I don't know where to begin. In my family a crisis was something you solved with cleaning products. I clear my desk in silence, while Umi goes to shut off the back-up generators and double-check that the fire escape is bolted. We herd Old Man Canary out the front door and into the snow.

Leaving? Canary says. No no no.

Yes yes yes, I say. Joe's going somewhere warm.

Canary's eyes light up. *Warm?* he says.

Sorry, I say, putting an arm around his shoulders. Not us.

We stand around while a pug-faced bloke welds steel bars across the door. The acetylene snarls and cracks. The surrounding factories and warehouses are locked and dark. Joe tries to give us money. I try to refuse but end up taking it. Canary starts shouting, and Joe gets upset and leaves without even shaking our hands. It all falls apart so quickly.

I sit in the snow and close my eyes and try not to think. Marie says it's one of my talents. I try not to think about her packed into the belly of the enormous army plane, holding Jordan close as the noise of the propellers rose to a howl. She could have gotten off, but she didn't. I hear Old Man Canary muttering as he wanders away somewhere, probably to die. Sleep rough these days, and in the morning they prise you off the footpath with a shovel. Umi's voice, talking on her phone, fades into the distance, and then there's just the wind blustering around the factory eaves.

I missed my flight for this.

Footsteps approach, and I open my eyes. It's Umi. She crouches at my side, her breath blowing clouds. I squint up at her.

Cheer up, she says, grinning. I've found somewhere we can go.

Sure, I say, my teeth chattering. The Harrods sale?

It's close by. And it's got a furnace.

There's nothing left to burn, Umi.

There's one thing left.

What?

Data. C'mon.

It sounds like she's lost her mind too. But there's a confidence in her voice that, right now, is as enticing as a hot bath. I stumble to my feet.

We only get as far as the back of the factory. Umi points to the wooden fire escape zigzagging up the wall. The door at the top is set in the old billboard, exactly where Margaret Thatcher's giant right eye should be. It looks like the Iron Lady's winking at us.

There, Umi says. I didn't check the fire door—I unlocked it.

It takes a second for this to register. Something leaps in me.

Oh my god, I say. We can go *in* the fire escape?

Yes. Joe left me to shut everything down. I just took out the fuses. We turn everything on and we're live.

What if he comes back? I ask.

Umi smiles. No one comes back. Except you.

We laugh, and I feel weak with relief. My brain's going *ohmygodohmygodohmygod*.

Umi boosts me, scrabbling and kicking, onto the bottom rung of the fire escape. I nearly lose my glasses. It's high and windy, the narrow stairs slick with ice. The whole dim sweep of the frozen docks falls away at my feet. It looks like the Thames is filled with ash. At the top I give the door a tug.

Bingo.

We step through Margaret Thatcher's eye socket and into her brain.

It doesn't take long to get everything back online. Umi replaces the fuses and throws the mains switch. Overhead lights ripple and snap on down the rows. The hard drives spin up, and the thousands of servers are soon chattering with life. Straight off there's a wave of heat from the exhaust vents.

We pull up chairs and sit with our hands held out to the warm air. Blood tingles in my thawing fingers. I keep stealing glances at Umi, her eyes gleaming in the light of the network traffic indicators. She's a little older than me, tall and solid and lively as a jackhammer. A jackhammer with a posh accent.

So far, so good, she says.

You're a genius, I say. We just run the place ourselves? Business as usual?

Not quite, she says, looking serious. This winter's going to be twice as bad as the last. We'll need a lot more heat.

But you can't buy heaters anymore, I say.

Heaters? Umi cries. She slaps a palm against the nearest server cabinet. What do you think these are? From now on this isn't a data centre, it's a data *furnace*.

A what?

Umi rubs her hands together. A data furnace. You know how much heat these things pump out. They spend billions cooling data centres everywhere else, but we want the heat. The more data we burn through them, the hotter they'll get. We boost the traffic and move in here, and I think we'll survive this winter just fine.

Move in? I say. You mean—together?

If you're staying.

I don't have a choice.

Then it's better with two of us. The building's secure, and we've got back-up generators if the power drops out. But we need to burn a seriously large amount of data to heat this place.

Then we need to make something that'll go viral, I say.

Exactly! Umi says. She pulls out her phone, and brings up the number one clip on YouTube.

It's a cranky old man from Blackpool trying to burn his heater. He dumps it in the fireplace and douses it with petrol. The flames get so big his ceiling catches fire. He runs round screaming *Oh my god! Barbara! Heat! Heat!* The talk shows wanted him, but I heard he died.

You know how obsessed people get with this stuff down in the drought belts, Umi says. These clips get millions of hits, and the bandwidth's all paid by advertising. That's what we need.

Millions of hits? I say. Us?

Umi grins. We'll think of something, she says, like it's the easiest thing in the world.

First we rearrange the servers to maximise their heat output. It takes a couple of weeks to lug the cabinets into tight concentric rings, vents facing inwards. Once we're done the place looks like an enormous futuristic hedge maze. We leave a space the size of a living room in the middle, and install our desks. I'm glad to finish each day exhausted. There's less chance I'll have to think.

When we're ready to move in, Umi helps me collect a few boxes of clothes and kitchen stuff from my place.

Which of these do you want? she says, looking at the photographs of Marie, Jordan and me on the hall table.

Ah, it's okay, I say. I've got some already.

Really?

Yeah. Anyway, they're much better looking in my head.

We load the boxes and my bed onto a sled, and drag it down Wapping High Street like some bizarre Icelandic wedding ritual.

Why didn't you get on that flight? Umi suddenly asks. Her cheeks are red with exertion.

I told you, I missed it, I say.

Bullshit. Umi stops pulling the sled. What happened, George?

I pretend to study a row of eviscerated council flats, standing beside the road like rotting teeth. I don't know, I say. Guess I couldn't bring myself to leave all this.

At the factory we place the bed in the centre of the

maze of servers. We sleep side by side, for warmth. After the months I spent sleeping alone in the spare room, woken only by Jordan's wails, Umi's breathing is a charm.

Day by day the temperature drops. We experiment with our own videos. The internet's going mad for footage of British animals snap-frozen into domestic poses. There's an ice-bound squirrel reclining next to a swimming pool, and a mummified kitten that looks like it's brushing its teeth.

When I find a dead sparrow in the back of a server cabinet, we stretch out its wings, attach it to a stick and film ourselves taking it out around the ruined city. Sparrow buys a sack of Charity Rice at the bulletproof Tescos. Sparrow hides from middle-class looters: management consultants and dentists in armoured snowmobiles. Sparrow goes scavenging through the ruined halls of the V&A, and falls in love with a stuffed partridge. In the end Umi films me launching the dead bird out the fire escape, into a blizzard.

Sometimes you just know when it's time to jump! I yell.

The clip doesn't get much traffic. Afterwards I feel mean.

Every last tree in the city's been burned, so there's nothing to suggest autumn, but it's clear summer has gone. Windblown snow sticks hard against the factory windows.

Soon daylight is just a brief translucence, and night after night I'm woken by the cold. I come up from a dream of Jordan, his newborn face spread beneath me like a landscape, veins branching through him like frozen rivers. Then he's gone, and there's just the drone of the fans and the thin streams of warm air, and a relentless chill on all sides.

Are you okay? Umi murmurs.

That's it, isn't it, I say. That's all the heat they've got.

She rolls to me. I'm not wearing my glasses, and her face is a soft blur.

They can punch out a lot more heat than this, she says. We just need something to really take off.

It's Joe's frog-in-the-pot thing, I say. Only in reverse. We're slowly freezing.

Umi doesn't reply.

We could put up a tent, I say.

What?

Put up a tent. Trap the heat, and sleep inside?

Sure, Umi says, but she isn't really listening.


In the morning Umi's gone, and she's not answering her phone. There's a pile of refugee-arrival printouts on my desk and a scribbled note: *You were talking in your sleep.* I stare down at them for a long time, then put them in a drawer to look at later. I lose the morning watching videos of a heat-deranged Canadian grizzly trying to eat a fishing boat.

Around three I hear the fire door. The wind whistles in off the river ice.

I've got it! Umi calls. Time to boost the traffic!

She crosses through the maze of servers, and places a large cardboard box on my desk. Beneath her frost-tangled fringe her face is radiant. She opens the box with a flourish. *Voila!*

Inisde is an ornate art-deco terrarium: a miniature world of pebbles, lush green plants, and a bowl of water. There's a handsome golden frog sitting in the water, his tiny chest shuttling in and out.

Where the hell did you get that? I ask.

British Museum of Natural History. They're evacuating this week.

I squeeze Umi's arm. That's brilliant.

Thanks. She beams.

Sarcasm, Umi. What on earth?

It's the frog in the pot! she cries. Put him in cold water, turn up the heat, see if he jumps, right? You'll love this.

She hefts the terrarium onto the server cabinet above our bed, then positions a high-resolution webcam. She opens her laptop and brings up the widescreen video of the terrarium in a browser. I can see the fronds on the ferns, the patterning of the frog's skin. Beyond, the server racks curve away into elegant soft focus. The old industrial machines loom like sentinels.

Beautiful, I say. But how's that going to boost traffic? And how are you going to heat the water?

Umi's jittery with excitement. Here, she says, indicating a graph beneath the video. That's the number of people watching. One for now: us. That's the power usage of the servers. And this one's the heat inside the terrarium. I've hooked up a sensor.

Oh no, I say. You're not.

Not what?

That's—sick! I'm laughing, and a little horrified. You've got the video of the frog hosted on the servers underneath the frog, right?

Right.

So—the more people watch the frog, the higher the load on the servers, the more heat they produce? It'll boil the water—people will cook it just by watching!

Yes! Umi says, clapping her hands. We spam out the link, and people have got to be curious. They visit the page, they push up the server load, the temperature goes up too. Incrementalism, I call it: billions of tiny, innocent actions that add up to catastrophe. Just like the real world.

Just like my marriage, I mutter.

What?

Nothing. So we just boil him to death and then, what, eat him?

Hardly, Umi says, frowning at me. He's tropical. We'd

need about a hundred thousand views an hour before he's in danger.

What are the chances? I don't want to be responsible for his death.

That's the beauty of it! No one's guilty. The responsibility'd be shared by about five million viewers.

But what if we really hit the big time?

I reckon Little George will jump.

Little *George*?

Umi smiles. A meme needs a name.

She's got all the answers. It's infuriating. There's a self-assurance planted so deep in her she doesn't even know it's there. A bit like a cancer, you could say. Only you wouldn't, if you were a small man living in very large times. Her confidence is all I've got.

Well, then, I say with a grin, Little George must be freezing.

Umi grins back. Shall we?

What the hell are we waiting for?


JUMP OR DIE. Umi's made a logo, with Little George lifting his head to ponder the question. We plaster it across every social-media channel we can find. I write press releases, and spend days spamming the link to stupid meme sites worldwide. I feel warmer just having something new to do.

By the end of the week four hundred people have tuned in. The temperature hasn't budged. At night we leave a lamp on beside the terrarium and climb into bed. It's beyond freezing.

If I wake up dead, I say, you have permission to burn me.

Umi puts an arm around my shoulder. Hey, she says. Most viral stuff takes weeks to get going. It won't happen overnight.


At eight I wake to the dull buzzing of my phone.

You the frog guy? How long do you give him?

There's whining static on the line. It's hard to hear. Who is this? I say.

Paul Sherman, *Sunday Mirror*. I saw your little stunt on fist-face.com. I'd like to do an interview.

What? When?

I'm out front.

Umi stirs beside me. Whatsit? she mumbles, and there's the same weird static over her voice. I realise it's the server fans running at a higher speed. People are watching. Lots of them.

Journo, I whisper, and her eyes blink open.

Haven't you been following it overnight? Sherman says in my ear. Where have you been?

Asleep.

Sleep when you're dead. Or when the frog's dead. Have a look.

I crawl to my desk and drag down my laptop. Goddamn, I say, exhaling slowly.

Two thousand, two hundred viewers. The graphs show an erratic climb. The temperature inside the terrarium is clocking thirty-four degrees Celsius.

I stand and cross to the terrarium with a duvet round my shoulders. Little George is sitting among the ferns with just his eyes visible. He looks like he's hiding.

Paul? I say. Come on up.


The story he runs is harsh: 'Heating Gimmick Animal Cruelty Shocker'. There's a photo of me and Umi looking smug, and a huge pull quote from the Royal Society for the Prevention of Cruelty to Animals: *This could be the first ever crowd-sourced execution. We strongly encourage people not to visit this website.*

My god, I say. People will hate us.

Exactly, Umi says. It's *perfect.*

She's right, of course. The article gets picked up by tabloids overseas as a those-crazy-freezing-Brits story. For the next few days traffic hovers at three thousand viewers an hour. It makes no difference to the icy air, but Little George paddles around happily enough.

Then an environmental magazine calls up and drills us

on the ideas behind the project. I start to tell the writer how it's a matter of life and death: we need to heat the factory to survive. Umi grabs the phone and starts ranting about how we're making a statement about society, industrialisation and the energy footprint of the internet.

It's garbage but the writer laps it up, and soon there's a string of stories about how we're trying to raise awareness about this or that. The internet doesn't give a shit. We get a real bump in traffic when the *Onion* runs with 'Young Brit Programmers Demonstrate Utter Futility of Human Civilization by Slowly Boiling Helpless Amphibian'.

For a fortnight we watch the numbers rise and fall. The days get shorter, and the northerly storms pound in. The silos beside the factory collapse into the street below, and the whole first floor vanishes under snow. A six-day blizzard closes London City Airport for good, and with it goes the last of the evacuation flights.

Inside the factory, Little George swims and eats and swims. The traffic is growing just fast enough to keep us from freezing. Umi stands behind my chair while I hit refresh like I've got a nervous tic.

This is the critical part, Umi says. She massages my shoulders with strong fingers. Right now we're on the cusp.


When there's a break in the weather one of us has to go out for supplies. I take my baseball bat and snowshoes, and prise open the fire door. The icebound city gleams. It's been weeks since I've felt the sun on my face. Snow is piled so high at the base of the fire escape that I can hop down from the third floor.

London had been grim in summer, but by now it has an austere beauty. I walk the towpath towards the bullet-proof Tescos. Glaciers have formed between buildings, and are calving tiny icebergs into the streets. The skyscrapers of Canary Wharf push up into the blue like a range of newly minted mountains. Snowdrifts have softened the lines of roads and buildings; everything that was once human now seems to belong to an ancient natural wilderness.

In the backstreets of Wapping a smell like roasting meat reaches me. Smoke rises from the chimney of an untouched terrace house: a cremation. A small traffic of mourners goes in and out, and from the house comes the melancholy chime of a hand bell. I remember going with Marie to the final memorial ringing of Big Ben. The great frozen bells had shattered like glass.

In the Tescos the fluoros flicker and buzz. Armed guards in black balaclavas watch me round the aisles. If they see me crying over the carrots, they say nothing. Marie used to shop here back when the shelves were full. Three per cent cheaper than Safeway, she liked to say. She'd evolved so perfectly to work the little levers of suburban life that when the shit really went down, it wrecked her. The Gulf Stream grinding into reverse, refugees like frightened cattle, riots outside Parliament, the layered snow an archive of spilled blood: it wrecked us both.

We watched the chaos on the news like it was happening somewhere else. Life kept getting worse, and we kept adjusting until we no longer recognised ourselves. Marie became a thin woman standing at the sink, waiting for a kettle which had already boiled. I became a man who told jokes.

That's all you do when you're upset, she said. Joke, joke, joke.

Bullshit, I said. Sometimes I clean the oven.

When she got pregnant she stopped talking. Something in her broke. Yet still I told her things would get better. I refused to give up hope.

I pack my purchases onto my sled, and dry my eyes so they don't freeze shut. As I drag the sled through the lobby, something catches my attention: two rheumy eyes peering from a nest of sleeping bags.

Canary! I yell.

Old Man Canary. I'd given him up for dead. The tip of his nose is eaten by frostbite, and when he manages a grin he's got even fewer teeth. His sparse grey beard looks like cobwebs.

How'd you like to go somewhere warm? I ask, crouching at his side.

*Warm?* he breathes.

He's not in good shape. I end up pulling him along

in the sled. We chatter away, me doing the talking, him throwing in his chirping monosyllables. I'm halfway through telling him about Umi's brilliant frog idea when he interrupts. It's the longest sentence I've ever heard him speak.

Told her yet?

Told who what? I ask, as if there was any doubt.

He grins.

By the time we reach home we're travelling in the dark. The windows across the back of the factory are ablaze, lighting the giant billboard like a beacon. Melt water runs down Maggie's face. A chunk of old ice slides from the roof and explodes into the snow.

Jesus, I say. Now we're cooking.

I help Canary slowly up the fire escape. We push open the door and it's like walking into a blast furnace. The heat is overwhelming, the exhaust fans so shrill it's hard to talk. In the flickering firelight of network traffic, the old industrial machines seem alive with the hiss and roar of steam.

Canary and I wend our way between the servers, shedding clothes as we go. My reflection paces me in the glass-fronted cabinets. I barely recognise my own skinny shanks, or the nervous hope on my face.

In the centre of the server maze Umi's at her laptop, dressed only in her underwear. Her long legs are propped on the desk, and I notice she's carefully painted her toenails fire-engine red.

Looking good! I say, trying not to stare.

Right back at you! she replies. You know the bookies are taking bets? Five to one he cooks. What do you think?

I think you should say hello to—

Oh my god! Canary! She crushes the old man's withered chest in a hug. How are you still alive?

Canary shrugs. He looks shy but proud.

Well, it's good to see you. Are you hungry? Did you get food?

I did, I say. But what the hell's happening here? How many viewers?

Smile, Umi says, nodding at the camera. You're live in front of thirty-two thousand viewers.

Thirty-two *thousand*?

It just jumped with your arrival.

My god. How's Little George doing?

He's in heaven.

I peer into the terrarium. The frog is kicking his back legs in lazy circles.

He seems fine, I say. But how on earth did we get so many—

*Wired*. They did a serious story, so now everyone else is taking the piss. It's pushing massive traffic our way. Check it out.

Umi runs through a series of windows on her laptop. There are a dozen parodies of our JUMP OR DIE logo, released within hours of the *Wired* story. Little George has been replaced with everything from kittens in toilet bowls to office workers atop the Twin Towers. There are people trying to make coffee on top of their servers and an NGO in the Hague crowd-boiling a lobster for charity.

Then the Korean barbecue restaurants caught on, Umi says. You cook your own food at your table and perform for the cameras. The more traffic, the hotter your barbecue. People do some wild stuff with sliced pork. Since then we've had three different crowd-boil kitten hoaxes, and now this. This is genius.

Umi maximises a live stream from three students in the San Diego enclave. They're already famous for posting videos of a stray cat that looks like Hitler. They've strapped Hitler cat to a miniature electric chair, attached a little helmet, and run a bunch of complicated wires down to the servers. Their traffic is going berserk.

The screen blanks. Umi hits refresh. Oh wow, she says. Their servers have been taken out.

Shit, I say. Crashed? Or hacked?

Dunno. But if they're offline, that's a million people looking for something to watch. We have to harness that.

Old Man Canary's grown bored of watching the screen. He's got his arms around one of the warm server cabinets, as if he'd like to dance with it.

Do we really need to boost our traffic? I ask Umi. This is pretty good.

If this is the peak, it's downhill from here, she says.

We've got to keep climbing.

But for how long? When do we pull the plug?

Later. Umi grabs my hand and holds it to her forehead. Feel that heat.

I brush her hair back off her face and tuck it behind her ear. Lovely, I say. But how long till he cooks?

Jump or die, Umi says with a grin. He'll jump.

I mean, how long before the water's hot enough to kill him?

Impossible to say.

Then shouldn't we shut this down? Before all that traffic finds us?

No way, Umi says. We need it.

But it'll push the load through the roof.

That's the point.

It'll kill him.

He'll jump.

He'll burn.

He'll jump. Of course he'll jump.

How can you be so sure? I demand. How can you be so fucking sure, *all the fucking time*?

Umi grins even wider. Animals are smarter than humans. There's no way he'll sit there and cook. It's simple.

Simple?

Simple, simple, simple.

Gah! I shout, and I grab her shoulders and shake them, and we're grappling, skin on skin, her self-satisfied lips

beaded with sweat, and I'm suddenly thinking about—
kissing her?

Kissing her.

On camera.

Sometimes you just know when it's time to jump.


Umi grits her teeth, and pulls away. Her face is shocked.

Oh, Canary says, eyes wide. *Cold*.

I'm turning from her, my heart a single ice cube, when, without warning, a traffic spike hits the factory like a physical force. The fans scream, the lights flicker and dim and the auxiliary generators roar to life like a row of diesel trucks.

Far out, Umi says. She's staring straight ahead at her laptop. CNN just posted our live stream to their entertainment page. That's mainstream viral.

Umi, I say. Sorry. I—

It's okay, she says. Blame the heat.

It kills me how quickly she accepts an apology. No, I say, I did—

Her smile is jammed on high. It's fine. It gave the traffic a good bump.

It's more than a bump: it's carnage. Within minutes JUMP OR DIE is trending all over. The comment feed is a blur of speculation and outrage. Still greater heat rushes the room, raking my skin and scorching into my lungs.

My mind fills with footage of the drought belts. That parched desolation. Defeat sitting behind the eyes like a bad hangover. I try not to think about where Marie and Jordan might have landed, and I fail. I know I have to get out of here.

Just walk away, I tell myself. You've already done it once.

By now we must be close to red-lining the system. Umi shakes her head every time I suggest we shut the servers down.

Later, she yells over the blast of the fans. It's only fifty-seven degrees in there. Heaps more capacity.

But what about Little George? I yell back.

In the camera shot, our heads loom above his terrarium like a pair of heat-stroked gods. I feel so faint I have to lean against the server cabinet, and I have the sudden woozy sensation that I'm back at Jordan's birth. Canary's taken off all his clothes. Umi's trawling back through all the mutations and parodies, looking for a way to tip this over into an internet-wide smash.

Sixty-two degrees.

Sixty-eight.

I try to summon anger, momentum. The tiny frog reaches the edge of the bowl and turns and circles round again.

Come on, you little bugger, I mumble. Jump.

He's okay, Umi says, and her voice sounds like it's

been slowed down. She's got a new parody of our logo up on the laptop screen. This time the image of the frog's been replaced with two naked figures. A strong, tall woman and a scrawny man, lips grotesquely puckered.

Fuck.

Superfuck.

I get it.

I take off my glasses, and I have to fight the urge to hurl them across the factory. I begin to laugh. It seems like such a good joke. Then I'm weeping.

I reach into the terrarium, and poke Little George. He sails away under my touch.

Careful! Umi says. He has to swim.

He's done, I say. We're making soup.

He's still moving.

The water's boiling, Umi. It's us.

What?

It's *us*. You think a hundred and fifty thousand people give a damn about a frog? They're all waiting to see what *we're* going to do. You and me, and Canary: jump or die.

I put my hands on her shoulders, and I feel her flinch. We're going to cook ourselves, I say. We have to shut this down.

She's staring over my shoulder. No way, she slurs. *More*.

I follow her gaze. It's Old Man Canary, and in the rising heat he smells terrible. Umi wrinkles her nose, then smiles.

Canary, she says. Old Man.

He takes my hand, and Umi's hand, and tugs. I realise he's got the fire door open. Already I can sense the air whipping in off the river ice, and it's the sweetest thing I've ever felt.

I gather my jackets, and through the heat-crazed air I see Umi hunting for her own clothes. At least I think that's what she's doing, until I see her dragging something into the centre of the servers. It's the fridge, from the kitchen.

With unbelievable strength she lowers two server cabinets onto their sides, then pivots the fridge so that it's lying on its back on top of the cabinets. She vanishes again.

Come on! I yell, turning to the door.

Canary's still standing in the centre of the maze, cloaked only in his green sleeping bag, fumbling with the zip. Umi returns with the fire hose. It only takes seconds to fill the upturned fridge. She retrains the webcam.

Umi! I yell from the doorway.

If she hears me, she shows no sign. I step out onto the first rung of the fire escape. Words are forming in my addled brain: a speech, a jumbled mess of a thing I've been putting off telling her since the day I came back to work.

Marie and I slept shoulder to shoulder on the stale airport carpet for a month, waiting for a flight to god knows where. I never gave up hope. But I woke one morning and saw her sitting with Jordan in her arms, perfectly still, watching the departure boards with such dumb patience that I realised she didn't care what happened. Hope, for her, was just another kind of resignation. They called our flight, and I told her I was going to the toilet. She didn't even ask why I was taking my bags.

As I walked away through the chaotic, stinking halls, past migration police with tasers and dogs, past the people at the bottom of bottomless lists, their heads lifting to hear the final call for my flight, I wasn't walking away from my son, or from my wife.

I was walking towards the one person I knew who had not lost hope, and would never lose hope, even if it killed her.

I throw my snowshoes out the fire escape into the white below. I take one last look at the world we've created—the server labyrinth ablaze with the internet's lunatic fire; the upturned fridge filled with water; Umi, grinning confidently, hands on Canary's shoulders, saying something I can't make out—and then I jump.

# SLICK

IN THE beginning, he was just a skinny guy named Simon working a bar in The Rocks. I'd covered my table with a spread of photos for a Kahlua ad I was working on. The model was a former Angolan child soldier turned pin-up girl. She had a boa constrictor wrapped around her, a rifle in one hand and a glass of Kahlua in the other. Her lips looked like they were about to disgorge something sexy and expensive. This guy brought me another Johnnie Blue and paused to survey the photographs. He looked like any other nervous hipster shithead in tight black Levis and Ray-Ban knockoffs till he opened his mouth. Jesus, he could talk. It was like being hit with a cattle prod.

Anorexia, he said.

Excuse me?

It's good, he said, but she's too plump. She looks normal. Starve her for a month and shoot it again—then it'll get interesting. Hell, starve the boa constrictor for a month as well. Then you'll sell some drinks.

Without waiting to be asked, he slid into the booth beside me, drank my whisky and bombarded me with questions about the advertising world. It was seriously dark in that bar but he kept his sunglasses on. He jumped chaotically from one topic to another and I remember thinking: he talks like a kid on a sugar high browses the net. I could barely keep up. Before I knew what I was doing, I'd taken him back to the office to meet Mary McGowan, our CEO. He took off his shades to reveal these strange pale-green eyes, crackling with bandwidth. He looked straight at Mary and smiled. She hired him on the spot.

For a while there, before we took over the world, life was much the same at the agency. I was solid, Slick was a whiz kid, but who cared? Advertising's full of these punks. They come on strong and burn out fast. Sure, his campaign for Audi showed talent. Leaving bullet-riddled A5 sedans outside foreign embassies sold a lot of cars. But Slick was from a family of see-you-in-hell Catholics from the western suburbs. All he'd had for stimulus was the Bible and the internet. I gave him a year, tops.

Then that BP rig blew a million litres of crude over the Gulf of Mexico's face. Birds and fish died in their millions, and whole towns and industries went belly-up. It was a public-relations disaster. When we came in one morning to find BP's Director of Global Marketing in the foyer, a ripple of excitement went round the office. This was going to be lucrative.

The BP guy was Jim Bacon. Most marketing directors are so cheerful you want to stab them. Jim looked old and tired. BP's stock had crashed, they were up for a trillion in federal damages and they'd had to stop advertising their green credentials in *National Geographic*. Worst of all, there was still a stinking black oil slick out there killing their business. They were desperate to clean up their image.

Jim told us he wanted a southern-hemisphere campaign to win support for their clean-up efforts. He'd liked our work for Audi. When he found out that was Slick's idea, he asked the kid to come in.

He's just a junior, I said.

Jim waved his hand. Bring him in.

Slick wandered into the boardroom and listened to what Jim had to say. Then he pushed his ridiculous lank fringe out of his face, looked Jim in the eye and started asking questions.

Who's doing your campaign in the States?

How's that working out so far?

What's your total budget?

What's your best-case scenario?

He listened to Jim's answers then said, like it was the most natural thing in the world: You need to fire all your other agencies, and give the whole campaign to us. You give it to us and we'll make that oil slick go away. It'll be the most ambitious campaign in the history of advertising. Ever.

For the next hour Slick outlined his plan. I don't know if he was making it up or channelling it from on high, but the rest of the world disappeared, and there was just Slick's voice and a weird electricity in the air.

The problem, he said, is that no one has ever gone all the way. People complain there's too much advertising. The problem is there isn't enough. Given what's possible, every campaign to date has been piecemeal and half-arsed. You might sell a few more toasters, but you quit before you've ever really started.

The secret is to expand your view of what's possible. We don't just do web or viral or TV or film or print or politics or bribes or school sponsorship, or whatever. We do all of them and more; we do things that haven't even been invented yet. No one will escape this campaign. It'll be an oil slick of information. With my ideas and the size of your budget we can make history. We can *unmake* history. Give the job to us and no one will ever remember there was an oil slick. No one. Not even you.

It was a hell of a pitch. We sat in silence. No one's iPhone rang. Jim Bacon's stunned expression thawed into a grin, and he nodded. He went into the hallway and made some calls. It was on.

After that, the madness. Our boardroom became a war room. We ate, slept and drank the oil slick. It started with a viral smear campaign *against* BP. The allegations were ingenious: napalm attacks on protest vessels, Blackwater contractors torturing seagulls and posting the photos to Facebook, political conspiracies we'd made up that later turned out to be true. We recruited, at one point, thirty-two per cent of all American college students to talk incoherently about the oil slick at parties. Slick even commissioned season six of *The Wire*, set in the Gulf of Mexico but without once mentioning the spill.

My strongest memory from this period is of the nightly strategy meetings. Come two a.m. you'd find a dozen of us at the boardroom table in our singlets, drinking Scotch and throwing round ideas. Slick watched over us with a beatific smile and a knowing twitch of the mouth.

Which option should we choose? we'd ask, and his answer was always the same.

All of them.

Two months in, something began to shift. Public opinion dipped, then rose a little, then plummeted. I started to worry. Petrol stations were bottled, yet share prices rose, and then a truckload of rotting sea turtles was dumped in the lobby of BP's New York headquarters. No one else at the agency seemed to care.

It's a *delicacy*, I overheard someone say on the phone. In Helsinki that shit is two hundred bucks a gobbet.

The rest of the team worshipped Slick, and the more incoherent public opinion looked, the happier Slick became. It made no sense. My questions became more and more shrill, and before I knew it Slick had put me in charge of a smear campaign against our own company. He was shutting me out. For months I picketed our front gate, chanting dumb slogans and linking arms with luddites, wondering what was happening inside.

Slick had changed too. He hadn't shaved in months and never seemed to sleep. At night, when security let me in after the day's protesting, I would pause in the doorway to watch him work. He sat at his bank of screens, humming with manic energy like he was in spiritual communion with the data. The numbers streamed past, reflected in his two-dollar shades.

One night he looked up and saw me.

Hey, he said gently. What's on your mind?

I swallowed, feeling ashamed, and angry that we'd let this child lead us so far astray.

It's all—this, I said, gesturing to the monitors and graphs. I don't understand what we're doing anymore. We've lost sight of the facts. Worse, we've lost sight of the *brand values*.

Slick took off his sunglasses and rubbed his eyes. He was skinnier than ever but his gaze was full of knowing kindness. I know you don't trust what we're doing, he said. That's okay. There are no brand values anymore, or facts. We're way past that. We're doing something revolutionary. These days we're so over-saturated that no single fact can mean a thing. So, what are we working with instead? Over-saturation itself. Creating it, shaping it—one giant ecosystem of chaotic over-stimulus. It's the new medium of communication. It's the only thing people can possibly understand.

He paused just long enough for me to blink in agreement.

Try not to think of it as an advertising campaign, he said. Think of it as an information mandala. Or a kind of magic-eye picture. Up close it looks like chaos, but as you draw back and the months pass and people try to make sense of it, they'll find a pattern. Their brains are hardwired to find meaning and, trust me, there is meaning in all of it. We'll buy the satellite imagery of the oil slick from space, maybe start a war in Mongolia, and launch a new Cormac McCarthy trilogy. Then it'll all come together. You watch.

I thanked him. Our eyes met and I tried to smile, but as I said good night my voice cracked. I was turning against him, and he knew it.

The campaign went into overdrive. We churned out daytime soap operas, claimed responsibility for Hurricane

Katrina and launched a new frozen yoghurt derived entirely from petrochemicals. I wanted to call it Oils Lick, but Slick said I was still thinking too literally. We routed half the world's internet traffic through Mexico and had mentions of disaster replaced by discussion about running shoes. We saturated people with so much gibberish they stopped noticing it was gibberish at all.

At the height of the craziness I answered a call from Jim Bacon. Get your boss, he croaked.

Mary took the phone. Beneath her make-up she blanched. Okay, she said. I'll call you back. She turned to the team.

Pack your bags, she said. You're not going to believe what's gone down.

That night six of us boarded a plane for the US. As the sky grew light over the Gulf of Mexico, we were watching from the deck of BP's research ship. Jim Bacon and his team of marketing execs stood grim-faced.

I'm not sure how to tell you this, Jim said, but—we've lost the oil slick.

What do you mean? one of our people asked.

Jim flung a hand out towards the horizon. See for yourself.

The sun slid into view. In front of us, the blackened remains of the oilrig stood silhouetted like a giant mechanical wading bird. Beyond was smooth ocean and the cries of seabirds, and a faint wind whistling in our ears.

How can you *lose* an oil slick? I said.

You tell me, Jim replied. We did as you asked and stopped the clean-up for a week, and when we got back out here we couldn't find it.

The deck erupted in shouting. Had the slick moved? Had it sunk? Somehow dispersed? Someone suggested we check the satellite data, but I pointed out that we'd already bought and changed it. Jim thought maybe BP's ship-towed chemical booms had finally worked, but we soon realised we'd made them up as well.

The buzz faded and died, and one by one we turned to look at Slick. He was leaned against the railing with his sunglasses on, watching us with a smirk.

All right, you, Mary said. Any thoughts?

We're done, Slick said.

All twelve of us on the deck stared at him.

It's over. We've won.

What do you mean? Jim said.

We did it. We made the oil slick go away. It's a work of freakin' art.

But where's the slick gone? I asked.

Slick shook his head, disappointed. They'll spend the next few weeks searching for the oil but they'll never find it—and eventually they'll forget about it altogether. We all will, and you know why? Because it never existed in the first place.

Slick looked at me.

There never was an oil slick, he said. That's what's at the heart of the mandala.

Let me get this straight, Jim said, a tentative awe in his voice. Your advertising campaign was so successful you've physically made the oil slick go away? It's just—gone?

Slick simply grinned. We stood there trying to let the idea sink in. Mary McGowan was leaned against the railing, crying. I went over and gave her a consoling hug but she shook me off. I saw she was crying with joy.

It's a fucking miracle, someone said.

But it doesn't make sense, I said.

The others scowled at me.

He's right, Slick said. We're way beyond making sense. He looked out towards the radiant dawn. We've finally broken through.


These long summer evenings when the mosquitoes whine, and sleep is a brand name I can't quite recall, I go walking. I unlock the back door and shuffle down to the beach. As I walk I replay that day in my mind. Does it weigh on my conscience? Does it grind me down?

It does. I betrayed him.

While the staffers danced, and a drunken Jim Bacon backflipped awkwardly off the side of the ship, I sat in a toilet cubicle staring at my phone. People needed to know the truth. I called the executive producer of *The View*, and for more than a few pieces of silver I spilled my guts.

Even as I rejoined the party, I knew I'd made a mistake. Jesus would never have been famous if he hadn't been crucified, and Slick—reclining in a deck chair, watching me with his infuriating smile—well, he knew it. It was the last time I saw him.

The party spread to the wrecked platform of the Deepwater Horizon. A few hours later, when my outraged voice began to blare from TVs around the world, Slick was nowhere to be found. A wildfire of bogus revelations blazed across the mediasphere. The agency was courted and maligned by everyone, from the climate sceptics to the Pope. British American Tobacco offered Mary a fortune to tackle cancer. Confusion was swift and total, and the truth—that thin thread, so easily lost—was but one hair in Slick's long and tangled beard. The man had disappeared.

Some evenings, if it's still early, I pass others strolling on the beach. To most I'm just a harmless old eccentric, Gucci slippers in hand. A few recognise me and there's hatred in their eyes. They think I did more than betray Slick.

*Murderer*, they hiss.

I shrug, and roll my cuffs, and amble on down the tide line. What really happened is nothing so banal.

Slick was the Messiah.

There. I've said it. The millennial doomsayers were right: He was coming. They were just looking in all the wrong places. The Messiah was a Bible-and-internet kid from Western Sydney, come again to walk this earth in jeans that were a little too tight. He ushered in a new spiritual age, and then returned to the network, from whence He came.

At the end of the beach I climb the steps to the headland. I sit and rest my bones, and light a cigarette—a great pleasure, as for some reason or other few of us used to smoke. The view over the Gulf of Mexico is wonderful from here. The ruin of the Deepwater Horizon stands majestic against the fading sky. These days people think it's a public sculpture, donated by BP. I know better.

I take a drag and sit forward, hands on knees, and stare out at the ocean. I'm very patient. If I stare long enough, and hard enough, like I was looking at a magic-eye picture, something begins to emerge from the chaos of tide and wind. There's something out there in the water, coating the waves from the horizon to the shore. It absorbs all light, and all life. When I close my eyes, the darkness behind my lids is not so dark as what's out there. I open them again, and it's gone.

# ARMS RACE

SAN FRANCISCO sparkled with life. Crowds of uniformed men and women poured through hooting, gridlocked streets. The cable cars were a heave of teenage drone pilots and good-time girls smashed on pheromones and Coke Zero Zero Zero. Flags flew from every house. Fireworks blossomed over the glassy reach of Mission Bay. Russia had joined the Allies, and it was official: the war was global. Everyone was in a great mood.

Alex Davidson felt like killing someone. She had a flight in an hour, and her cab had been stuck in traffic for so long that she wasn't far off walking to the airport. That, or setting fire to the enormous billboards of General Hurtz lining the roads. It'd be the most productive thing she'd done all week. Her film crew was heading home after spending one last, infuriating day cornering drone pilots outside Sweeney Ridge Base. The pilots had turned it into a game.

Alex: What do you say to suggestions that General Hurtz is covering up civilian casualties in the conflict zone?

Pilot: That's an important question, and we've been discussing it a lot on the base. In all honesty, I believe— that you should show us your tits.

Six hours of that, and the shooting budget for her documentary was finally gone. The producers expected her home the next day to begin editing. She pressed a hand to her temples.

You all right? the cabbie asked, eyeing her in the mirror.

Headache, she said. Nothing a bullet wouldn't fix.

Do what you feel, the man said.

Up ahead, a crowd of drunken pilots came capering through the stopped traffic, singing and drumming on car roofs. One of them stuck his head through Alex's cab window. Hey, baby! he yelled. You're gorgeous!

His friend jostled in beside him, and his face lit up. Hey! Didn't you used to be famous?

Alex screwed up her face like she was sucking a lemon. She'd mastered the expression for these situations. Maybe I look like someone else?

Yeah, maybe, the man said uncertainly. You look a bit like that newsreader. You know, the one that had a meltdown on air?

Beats me.

Said all kinds of crazy stuff about General Hurtz? Called her a traitor? Wanted to stop the war?

Wrong woman, Alex said. I prefer to start wars.

Cool, the man said, grinning. Well, just so you know, you're easily beautiful enough to be on TV.

Thanks, Alex said, turning her widescreen smile on the man. That's very kind. And just so you know, you guys are easily dumb enough to be castrated.

The man's grin vanished. Come here and try, he said.

Alex opened the door and stepped out. She was six foot one even before the spike heels, with hacked black hair and huge owl eyes. She towered over them.

Bitch, the man said, backing away.

Yeah, the other said. Suck my dick.


Alex reached her check-in counter in time to see the screens change from NOW BOARDING to FLIGHT CLOSED. Her fury rose another notch. Off-duty pilots still streamed through the personnel line, clutching bottles of bourbon and half-eaten roast chickens.

What about them? she said.

The prim young woman at Alex's counter wouldn't even look up from her screen. I'm so sorry, ma'am, she said again. The flight is now *extremely* closed.

I'll yell fire, Alex said casually, just to see what

the woman would do.

She finally looked up from her screen, and did a double take. Hey, she said. Didn't you used to be famous? Like, on TV?

Alex let her face slump like an undercooked cake. I wanted to be on TV, she said. But my boyfriend kept me locked in a shed.

Uh, right, the woman said. Is he still your boyfriend?

No, Alex said. Now he's my husband. How about getting me on that flight?

I'm so sorry, ma'am. There's nothing I can do about that.

Nothing at all?

I'm so, *so* sorry.

The woman didn't look sorry.

Oh, forget it, Alex said. You're a peasant. Peasants have been powerless throughout history.

The woman blinked in surprise. Well, I have the power to book you another flight?

That's better, Alex said. Get me on the next flight to Mongolia.

Ha ha, the woman said.

I'm serious.

But—there's a war on, you know? In Mongolia. It's hell in there.

What? No.

Yes. Where have you been? Drone on drone? *Support*

*Our Boys Who Are Still Here*? Work-From-Home Guard? We've been fighting China for the last—

I know, Alex said sweetly. I'm making a documentary about it. Isn't it a shame we don't send peasants off to be slaughtered anymore?

Um, I guess, the woman said. I'm really sorry about—

Alex yanked up the handle of her case and headed for the exit.


It took another two-hour taxi ride to get back into central San Francisco. The streets were still jammed with revellers. Alex hadn't eaten since breakfast. The way she felt right now, even the war zone in Mongolia had to be better than this. She wound down her window and took a breath and screamed her frustration at the passing crowds. They cheered and waved right back.

In Chinatown, Alex checked into a hotel, then walked through the crowds to a noisy flag-draped pub with the intention of getting blind drunk.

Over a counter meal she sank a bottle of red and tried not to watch the news. Russia had finally sided with the US. With their support the 75th Deskbound had retaken the Mongolian capital in heavy fighting: two hundred drones lost, eight billion dollars wiped from the army's stocks. The footage was spectacularly entertaining. Fighter drones spiralled through the concrete canyons of the Ulan

Batuur financial district. Cluster bombs bloomed across the city grid. Alex eyed the drunks cheering along the bar.

This damn war, said a lazy drawling voice. Everyone so fucking cheerful.

Alex glanced at the man in the neighbouring seat. He looked like an off-brand pimp: flat-brimmed cap, puffer jacket and cheap gold chains. He was staring at the crowd with disgust.

You're a rare one, Alex said. I thought cynics were drowned at birth.

Round here, maybe, the man said. Drop you on your head, where I'm from. He paused, narrowing his sharp almond-shaped eyes. Say, don't I know you from someplace?

Alex shifted her features into a look of delight. I fucked your mother, she said. Pass me a napkin, son.

The man burst out laughing. Alex turned back to the screen.

They had yet another new woman reading the news. She sat there sweetly reciting the body counts. *Us, Them, Civilians. Zero, Zero, Zero.* Half the bar chanted along in unison. *Zero, Zero, Zero.* They finished every bulletin with that mantra. The newsreader smiled at the camera. She was stunning. Alex ordered another bottle of wine.

The door to the pub blew open and a herd of school kids in khaki overalls trampled in. They pushed in along the bar like suckling piglets. The nearest, a myopic boy with red hair and hunched bones, was practically climbing over Alex trying to get the bartender's attention.

Bit young, aren't they? she said to the man next to her.

He smiled. You make 'em fight—you gotta let 'em drink.

What? They're drone pilots?

Ask him.

The kid's eyes were crazed with adrenalin and booze. Yeah, he said. Fighter drones. Just back from the battle for UB. It was…Hey, didn't you used to be famous?

Yes, Alex said. I just got out of prison for molesting children. How can you be a pilot? You're not eighteen.

They dropped conscription to fourteen on Tuesday, the kid said. Faster reflexes.

Alex reached out and pinched the kid, hard.

Ouch! Fuck!

You're not that fast, Alex said. Going to war at your age?

*We're* not hurting anyone, the kid said, rubbing his arm. Mongolia's totally cleared of people. We're just blowing up chink drones.

Well, then, Alex said. You deserve a beer.

You buying?

You getting a pilot's wage?

The kid grinned. Yeah.

Buy your own fucking drinks, Alex said.

The kid slunk off, and Alex's neighbour barked with

laughter, his chains jingling like sleigh bells. Damn, he said. You just bitch-slapped a child.

No drunk toddler fucks with me, Alex said with a dewy smile.

Around them, the crowd simmered down to watch General Hurtz's nightly address. Her authoritative soccer-mom face beamed out from screens on every wall. The woman looked uncannily like Sarah Palin, with gold-rimmed glasses and a neat brunette bob. Alex grimaced. She'd spent so many hours reviewing footage of Hurtz that the general's face kept cropping up in her dreams.

I think we all agree that the new warfare *is* expensive, Hurtz was saying, but it's worth every cent. Take collateral damage. That used to mean drones, Hellfire missiles, dead civilians. Under my command collateral damage is just moving folk out of the war zone so they stay safe and sound. Every resettled Mongolian family's guaranteed a house of their own. Eighteen months of fighting and we haven't had a single casualty. Would you put a price on—

Ain't Hurtz a goddamn genius? Alex's neighbour said.

No, Alex said.

The man's eyes went mock-wide. No?

No. She's a rat-shit barber weasel.

You can't say that.

Alex leaned in confidentially. Rat. Shit. Barber. Weasel. Fucked in the ass by a unicorn.

Ha! the man said, pushing his cap back on his head.

I just worked out who you are. You're that lady that had a freakout on TV! Got stuck into Hurtz. That was dope!

Alex put her face in neutral. No one had reacted like that before. Dope? she said.

Yeah, dope, the man said, eyeing her dishevelled Armani blazer. You still dress like a newsreader. But what's with your face? If you don't mind me sayin', your expressions— they *wrong.*

Alex let idiot sincerity flood her eyes. That better?

Whoa, the man said, pulling back. How you do that?

That's the newsreader's job, Alex said, making herself go cross-eyed. Always having the right reaction. Now I have the wrong reaction.

Fair nuff. So what the fuck happened that night?

From what I remember, Alex said, I poured my drink in your lap, smashed my glass on the bar and stabbed you in the eye.

Right, the man said. Forget I asked. What you doing these days?

Alex sighed. She raised her fingers into scare quotes. Being a 'real' journalist. Making a documentary about Mongolia.

Oh, lemme guess, the man said, his face darkening. You another brave journalist doing another brave story 'bout the lucky Mongolians so you can win a prize for your brave-assed self. You should get a Pulitzer. You should be taken out back and given a good hard Pulitzering.

Easy, tiger, Alex said. I'm making a serious film, about Hurtz and the war. You've heard the rumours, right?

The man nodded warily over the top of his beer. I heard she has three breasts.

Alex snorted. I'm talking about casualties. You can't have war without bodies. Hurtz's Zero Zero Zero thing's got to be bullshit.

Sorry, lady, the man said. Ain't nothin' left there to kill.

What would you know?

What would *I* know? the man said. The fuck I look like to you? Kazakhstani?

What? You're Mongolian?

No, I'm Swedish. Go on, ask me about Genghis Khan.

What?

Nothing. Forget it.

Shit, sorry, Alex said. But your accent?

Baltimore, the man said. Went there to do fucken business studies, been there ever since. No home to go home to.

Damn, Alex said. You got family here?

Nope. In the resettlement camps, Chinese side.

I'm really sorry. Can I—buy you a drink?

Still wanna stab me in the eye?

Only a little bit, she said, holding out her hand. Peace? I'm Alex.

The man looked at her, and his broad face relaxed into a smile. Aight, peace, he said. Call me Marlow.

Alex waved the bartender over. On screen, the

president was handing out Purple Heart medals to wounded pilots. *First Lieutenant Susan Wilkie, repetitive strain injury. First Lieutenant Bernard Wolfowitcz, repetitive strain injury. First Lieutenant Claire O'Neill, acute repetitive strain injury.*

So, tell me 'bout this film, Marlow said. What's it called?

You'll love this, Alex said. My producers want to call it *Truth, Accountability, Democracy: Zero, Zero, Zero.*

Sounds wild. When's it out?

I don't know, Alex replied. Probably never.

As she said it, something unpleasant fell into place. She'd officially finished filming, but with the footage she had there was no way she could make a credible documentary. No wonder she was so damn wound up.

It feels un-fucking-finishable, she said. I've got nothing.

Aww, Marlow said. You still got a country. Why can't you finish it?

The film's about General Hurtz but I can't get near her. She only does pre-records by satellite; no one even knows where she's based. And the footage I've got that suggests bodies on the ground? Blurry freeze-frames from official army feeds. There's no independent coverage.

For real, Marlow said. I heard they shoot the news drones down.

Reuters, AP, boom. I've got experts, conspiracy

theorists, all the usual junk, but editing that's deckchairs on the Titanic. Without on-the-ground proof the film's a joke. I'm going to humiliate myself.

Again, Marlow said nonchalantly.

Alex laughed. You're about as charming as I am.

Marlow took a swig of beer. So why don't you just go?

Go where?

Mongolia.

Oh, sure, Alex said. I'd love to be the first casualty of the whole damn war.

Go on then.

After the day I've just had? Why not?

Great. Need an interpreter?

No, my Mongolian's perfect. But come anyway—you can get killed, I'll film.

It's the western way, Marlow said. At least get your ass to the Russian border, take a look around. From today they're allies, right?

True, Alex said. Nothing better to do. Finish our drinks and go?

Aight. Cheers.

Cheers.

They clinked glasses, and Alex downed her wine in a gulp. She looked along the bar, and found General Hurtz looking back at her: from the banners around the walls, the TV screens, even the beer coasters. Alex put a drunken hand on Marlow's shoulder.

You're kidding, aren't you? she asked. About going to Mongolia?

Not really, Marlow said.

Alex smiled. Neither am I.

Three weeks later, as they headed down the corridor towards the plane, Alex was terrified. It reminded her of her first day at NTV, walking from hair and make-up to the set. She hadn't even finished her journalism degree and she was about to go live in front of millions of people. The psychotically cheerful faces of staffers drifted past. *You look amazing!* they kept telling her. She'd beamed, but had to keep telling herself: *That's not why they hired me.*

Things went smoothly with Russian immigration. Alex had told the visa office they were going to interview Mongolian refugees along the border. She'd told everyone else she was taking stress leave in Hawaii.

Fantastic idea, her executive producer had said. Take a week or two for yourself. You've been a little—wound up of late.

You've been a right bitch, her elderly mother had said. Give this Hurtz business a rest; you're wasting your youth. Go lie on a beach and find yourself a man.

Sure, Mom, she'd replied. I'll send you his head.

On the ground in Vladivostok they found an army-surplus store and loaded up with serious snow gear, rations, flak jackets and steel helmets. Then they took a connecting flight to Irkutsk. At Marlow's insistence they hired an ancient white Hummer. He opened the rear passenger door and climbed in.

What am I, your fucking chauffeur? Alex said.

Play with me, he said, handing her a CD. Put this on.

What is it?

Music, Moneypenny. Crank it.

Alex slid the CD into the changer. A banging hip-hop beat filled the airport car park. The guttural harmonics of Mongolian throat-singing floated over the top.

Nice, Marlow drawled. Real nice. He wound down the window and gave the parking attendant an imperious nod. Now drive.

They rumbled south down the B32, past the smoke-stacked skylines of industrial towns, then turned at Ulan Ude onto broken back roads. Even here the highways were lined with billboards of General Hurtz, smiling beneath the slogan ZERO ZERO ZERO. They began to see distant drone flights shuttling across the horizon. The whine of engines reached them on the chill breeze.

So, how you wanna play this? Marlow said. There are about a dozen camps along this stretch of border.

Alex shrugged. Start by asking around. If there's a way across, someone here'll know.

The First Mongolian Neighbourhood Resettlement was a rough encampment strung along the road like an impoverished strip mall. Skinny dogs scattered and regrouped behind the Hummer. Children watched from doorways with wary curiosity.

In the centre of the settlement was a muddy car park, bordered by rows of houses built from shipping containers. Three American army trucks were pulled to one side. A shouting match was in progress. Half a dozen soldiers faced off against a crowd of Mongolian men with tired faces and proud bellies.

What the hell do you think these are? one of the soldiers was shouting. He scythed his arm at the shipping containers. Exactly what you were promised: a house of your fucking own!

No! the Mongolians chorused back in thick accents. *House! House* of your own!

Yes! For Christ's sake. House of your own!

No! *House* of your own! the Mongolians shouted.

One of the younger locals set off around the car park in a skipping trot, his hands raised like rabbit paws. He made strange high-pitched sounds.

The soldiers groaned and swore and threw up their hands. Why do you keep doing that? Would you please stop fucking doing that!

Marlow and Alex jumped down from the cab. The group paused to watch them approach: Alex in snow fatigues and combat boots, her short black hair in a severe twenties part; Marlow in a full-length fur coat.

Who the hell are you? demanded a stocky, harassed-looking woman wearing a captain's insignia.

Reporter, Alex said, flashing her press ID. This is my interpreter, Marlow. What's going on?

Ain't supposed to talk to reporters, the captain said. But say, didn't you used to be famous?

That'd be my sister, Alex said. She died in a waterskiing accident. Can you tell us what's happening, off the record?

Off the record? The captain ran a hand through her hair. Well, sure. You remember General Hurtz's promise—every relocated Mong family gets a house of their own? Well, we brought every last motherfucker here a house, and guess what? They don't want 'em. But look at 'em. They still standing here, screaming they want a house. Fools don't make no sense.

Hey, sister, Marlow said. You got an interpreter?

Sure, the captain said, holding up a small screen. Google Translate. Ninety-eight per cent accurate.

That ain't an interpreter, Marlow said. Let me ask what's going on.

He exchanged a quick burst of Mongolian with the men, then turned away and erupted in a fit of coughing.

Jesus, Alex said. Are you okay?

Translator, Marlow gurgled. *House.*

What the hell's up with him? the captain asked.

He's just emotional, Alex said. Can I have a look at your translator?

172

Sure.

Alex took it and read. There, she said, tapping the screen. There's your two per cent.

The captain screamed with exasperation.

What's wrong? the soldiers asked, fingering their guns.

Translator got it wrong, the captain moaned. Not houses, *horses*. They're fucken nomads. They all thought they were getting a *horse* of their own.

A volatile silence filled the car park. Alex bit her lip.

Come on, the captain said. We gotta send this upstairs.

They turned and walked dejectedly to their trucks. Alex rolled her eyes at the Mongolians. No English, huh? she said.

The men ignored her and stood quietly watching. The soldiers climbed into their trucks. When the last one pulled from the parking lot, the men screamed with laughter, howling and collapsing into each other like drunken wrestlers.

Plenty English, one of the men gasped. Do more horse, Ganzorig.

The young man set off again, trotting and neighing. He was laughing so hard he fell over in the snow. Another man staggered over and urinated on Ganzorig's boots.

My horse piss on your house! he yelled.

They laughed together, and the men pressed forward to shake hands. The scent of vodka and wood smoke filled Alex's nostrils. Ganzorig and Marlow spoke at length.

Have they heard anything about the rumours that General Hurtz is based along this stretch of border? Alex said.

Marlow translated, and turned back to Alex with a smile. That guy there with the belly says Hurtz's a ghost who comes in the night to steal their children. Ganzorig says she's a capitalist who comes in the night to steal their country.

Tell them I had no idea they were going to be so boring, Alex said. What about the body count? Do they know anyone who's missing?

The men shook their heads in response to Marlow's translation.

Try not to look disappointed, he murmured to Alex.

Sorry, she said. One more question—do they know of anyone crossing into Mongolia?

Again Marlow translated, and the men smiled grimly. Ganzorig said something that made the others smirk.

What'd he say? Alex asked.

The closest would be 'kaboom', Marlow said.

Come on, Alex said, miming the up-and-over action of crossing the border. There's got to be a way.

Ganzorig copied her mime, but swooped his other hand down like a drone.

Like, *totally* kaboom, he said in English.

Alex wondered what it would be like to be strafed from the air—and a faint hissing sound rose into a deafening scream as a squadron of fighter drones tore overhead.

She ducked, the drums of adrenalin commanding her to run. When she raised her head the men's faces were stony.

Ganzorig nodded at Alex, and spoke in Mongolian.

He's confused, Marlow relayed. Says you don't *look* suicidal. Haven't you seen the news? Mongolia's a smoking crater.

Everyone's seen the news, Alex said. Has anyone seen it with their own eyes?

They've seen plenty, Marlow said. There's a lookout. Ganzorig says he'll give us directions.

Alex pulled the truck onto the main road. They sped east to the sound of Mongolian hip-hop. The road grew steep, winding above a deep river gorge, and they found themselves stuck behind a line of stately black station wagons.

Oh my god, Alex said. No bodies? This looks like a mass funeral procession. Grab the camera.

Marlow leaned out the window to film as Alex pulled alongside. The drivers were ordinary Mongolians, the enormous car trunks jammed with turnips and lolling pigs. Marlow yelled something, and one of the drivers yelled back. Marlow roared with laughter.

What's going on? Alex said.

This lot thought they were getting horses too.

And instead they got—

Ninety-eight per cent, baby! Left here.

Alex swung the Hummer onto a rutted dirt track. Windows down, stereo booming, the truck climbed out of the valley to reach a lookout high on the ridge. Through a break in the trees they saw a jumble of saw-toothed hills receding south. The land was black and burned: a postcard defaced by war. One range still smouldered with fires.

Alex shut off the truck, and there was just the sound of the wind.

And there she is, Marlow said. Our fair smokin' motherland.

How long since you've been back? Alex asked.

Three years. Look at it—those motherfuckers.

Marlow jumped down and slammed the door. Alex filmed as he crossed to a cairn of heaped stones draped in brilliant blue rags. He stood for a long time, then pulled out a crumpled pack of cigarettes and tossed it onto the pile.

Quitting? she called.

An offering to the sky gods, he said, removing his hat. The old ones. Here come the new ones.

The blat of a surveillance drone ricocheted across the valley. The tiny unmanned aircraft turned and circled overhead, its cross-shaped shadow passing back and forth over the clearing. Alex stared up at it, fascinated to see a drone in the flesh.

What's it doing? she asked.

Won't know till it's done it, Marlow murmured. Don't move.

For several minutes the drone hovered. The whine of its rotors defeated all thought. Alex's fascination faded, and she felt fear and obedience building in her chest. She watched the sun dropping in the west, the sky thickening with high cloud. Distant fires took on the arachnid gleam of eyes. Another drone came in fast and low across the valley, then two more in quick succession. The four craft circled like buzzards.

This don't feel right, Marlow said.

A searchlight snapped on, and Alex's stomach shrank. A speaker mounted beneath the first drone crackled to life.

ATTENTION, ATTENTION, a voice commanded.

Alex and Marlow craned up, squinting against the light.

MA'AM, the voice said. DIDN'T YOU USED TO BE FAMOUS?

Alex blinked in surprise. Yes, she shouted. I did.

DID WE MEET IN THE PUB IN SAN FRANCISCO?

What the hell? Alex shouted. That you, kid? With the fast reflexes?

SEE, TOLD YOU GUYS IT WAS HER!

The drones' rotors slowed, and the four craft drifted down into a bobbing semicircle. Alex narrowed her eyes against the stinging downdraught. The fading sun was reflected in each drone's front camera.

MA'AM? the kid said. I HAVE A REQUEST FROM OUR FLIGHT COMMANDER.

There was a pause, then a snigger.

SHOW US YOUR TITS!

Alex seized a rock from the pile and hurled it as hard as she could. Piss off! she yelled. You little shit! All of you. Get the hell out of here!

The searchlight snapped off and the four craft lifted away, trailing obnoxious laughter. Marlow was bent double.

Oh, you too? Alex demanded. Hilarious.

Sorry, sister, Marlow wheezed. Peace. I'm just laughing 'cause I'm scared.


They camped at the lookout. Alex gathered firewood in a rage. Marlow sat out of the wind with his hood up, watching her and smoking. Every few minutes a drone flight scorched overhead.

You still want to walk in there? Marlow said.

Alex ignored him. She lit the kindling.

Marlow grinned. You do, don't you? He crossed to the truck and returned with his pack. He dug out a bottle of vodka. They got a name for people like you in Baltimore.

What's that?

Dead. Here.

Alex unscrewed the cap and took a shuddering mouthful. I'm going to find that kid and spit roast him, she said, coughing.

No doubt. But out there? Who's gonna survive that?

The wind was gusting now, bringing a brutal chill

from the north. Snow flurries settled into the fire with a wet hiss. Alex chewed her salt-flavoured army rations and swigged from the bottle in silence.

First real snow, Marlow said. If the drones don't kill us, we'll freeze. Or the wild animals'll eat us.

The ghostly glow of another flyover lit the clouds. A series of flashes lit the valley below, and a rolling boom swept through the campsite.

C'mon now, girl, Marlow said. I wanna blow this wide open as much as you do, but we gotta stick to the camps. You're too beautiful to get yourself killed out there.

Alex thrust out her front teeth like a beaver. And if I looked like this? Straight to the slaughter?

I'm kidding.

Yeah, yeah, can't take a joke. Alex took another slug of the vodka. What the hell's beauty got to do with anything?

It's how you got your job on TV, right?

Fuck off, Alex said. I studied at Columbia.

Aww, Marlow said. Oppressed by beauty. FPW, girl.

What?

First World Problem.

Dumbass, Alex said. FPW would be First Problem World.

Whatever. You know, I was watching NTV the night you blew it.

Through the vodka and the cold, Alex felt her skin prickle.

What went wrong? Marlow said. You were looking so good. You made such a mess.

Alex closed her eyes. She'd been fighting with the producers for months. They vetoed every story she put forward about conflict with China. They were happy to broadcast the president speaking of peace when, to many, the signs pointed to war. There was constant friction over air-defence zones in the Pacific and North Asia. General Hurtz, a complete unknown, was appointed CEO of the Armed Forces, and military spending went through the roof. Preschools received donations of ultra-realistic flight simulators. Both the Americans and the Chinese began drone exercises in Mongolia. Then it was more than exercises; Mongolians began flooding over the Russian border. How could the network not run stories about going to war?

Because we haven't *gone* to war, the executive producer shouted. I don't want to hear another fucking word about Hurtz and the coming apocalypse. I do not pay you to speculate. I do not even pay you to be a journalist, because you are not a fucking journalist. I pay you to sit, look good, and read exactly what we put in front of you. *Ex-act-ly*. So let's get to it.

Alex took her place on set. One minute until she was live in front of sixty million people. All her friends and family, every stranger she was ever likely to meet. Sit. Look good. Read.

There was commotion in the control room. She could

see them flapping in her peripheral vision. Not a fucking journalist, huh?

Thirty seconds. Cameras one and two fired up. Could she just recite a story about Hurtz and the coming war from memory? She would choke if she ad-libbed. Once they went live she was on autopilot. She was a drone.

Ten seconds. Brassy theme music flooded the set. There was sudden chatter on the crew-only channel. The cameramen were listening intently. One of them choked on his coffee. Two seconds. The autocue began its relentless glide. Alex blanked her mind and lit her smile. They were live.

*Good evening. Welcome to NTV News, I'm Alexandra Davidson. President West today returned from day five of joint friendship talks in Beijing—*

She read without registering a word. It took total concentration to maintain her composure, her famous sparkling eyes. Her voice was a bottomless well of empathy. She read about the mid-term run-off in Maryland. She read about firestorms in Australia. She read about fears of a viral outbreak in the Pacific. The next story rolled up on the autocue.

*Speculation is mounting that America and China are preparing for large-scale drone hostilities in*

*North Asia. Following tension between Washington and Beijing over resource allocation, trade tariffs and cattle exfoliation, sources in the Department of Defense point to a threefold increase in spending on unmanned aerial circus, in response to China's expansion of military cutlery into their northern steaks.*

There was something wrong with the autocue. Alex dimly noted that one of the cameramen had fallen over. She pushed on.

*China has responded by erecting a series of preposterous tents, including the desecration of a bilateral mermaid, and the retooling of US wing nuts held by Chinese foals. Department sources name General Hurtz as the traitor behind this—*

They were sabotaging her. People would forget she was reading an autocue and assume she'd lost her mind. The second she choked they'd cut to a commercial break and fire her on the spot. But her training was good: the expressive dance of her eyebrows never faltered, and her voice ran true. An incredulous silence took hold on set. Alex calmly read on, even as the autocue gave up all pretence of a news story and collapsed into a foul swill of Celine Dion lyrics, fragments of Hitler's speeches, rejected dialogue from *Avatar* and jokes from far-right chat rooms, before disintegrating into a string of binary code that seemed to run forever.

*Zero.*

*One.*

*One.*

*Zero.*

*One.*

*Zero.*

*Zero.*

*Zero.*

*Zero.*

*One.*

*Zero.*

*One.*

*Zero.*

*One.*

*One.*

*Zero.*

*One.*

*Zero.*

*Zero.*

*One.*

*One.*

*Zero.*

*Zero.*

*Zero.*

Alex snapped.

You pigs, she screamed into camera one. You pigs! We're going to fucking war!

The lights went out.


Alex stood unsteadily. She dropped the vodka bottle. She felt like she'd swallowed a fistful of dirty snow. Cold, she mumbled. Putting up the tent.

Better sleep in the truck, yo, Marlow said. Warmer.

She stumbled over to the truck, and flung open the back door. All yours, she said. I'm tenting by myself.

You wanna freeze to death? Marlow said.

No, that's your job, Alex said. She yanked her heavy pack down from the Hummer and slammed the door. I'll be camped over here.

She stalked off into the trees. The snow was coming in thick and soft now, the dark earth turning to an even white.

ATTENTION, ATTENTION.

Alex froze.

EXCUSE ME, MA'AM.

She turned back to the fire. It was Marlow, drunk, helpless with laughter.

SHOW US YOUR TITS!

Hey! Fuck you! Alex shouted, but the wind snatched her voice away. She turned and walked faster. Screw that bullshit ghetto nomad prick. She hoped he froze to death.

And screw that runt kid and his pervert mates and whoever put children in charge of that sort of firepower, and the whole insane war—and screw the NTV producers: not a fucking journalist, huh?—and screw her friends, the bastards, telling her to stay home, keep her head down, vanish, die, as if being embarrassed was the problem, and while she was at it screw her parents too, making half-assed soothing noises like demented pigeons when it was obvious, it was so fucking obvious, they hated that she wouldn't leave it alone. Screw every last goddamn one of them.

Alex halted her march. She'd forgotten what she was doing. What the hell was she doing? Looking for a campsite. In a blizzard.

She turned slowly. By the beam of her head torch the world was just a ragged circle of tree trunks and steep, snowy ground. Through her fury, and the false and viscous warmth of the vodka, she registered an urgent signalling. She was freezing. She had no idea where the truck was. Her tracks were just a faint disturbance, growing fainter all the while.

Alex dug more layers from her pack, strapped on snowshoes and set off into the blizzard, quickly now. For what felt like hours she followed her prints back towards the truck. Twice she paused, terrified, certain she'd heard someone shouting over the wind.

There's no one there, she told herself. Keep moving. You'll freeze if you stop. Just follow the tracks. Don't stop.

She stopped. There were no tracks anymore. Her brain was linking random humps and hollows. She was exhausted and cold and lost.

*Shelter, dumbass*, said a voice inside her.

Alex staked down the tent, rolled out her sleeping mat, climbed into her down bag, cracked a chemical heat pack and turned off the torch. She lay there, exhausted.

Show us your fucking tits, she muttered.

Sleep came swiftly down.


Alex woke, sore but warm, in the muted glow of dawn. She groaned: that was a lot of vodka. The walls of the tent pressed close beneath a weight of snow. She lay and listened. Nothing. Just the crisp silence that follows a blizzard.

Alex sat up. There was someone curled next to her in the tent. She screamed.

Oh my god, Marlow groaned, rolling over in his sleeping bag. His face was chapped and red from wind-burn. You still trying to kill me?

What the hell? Alex said.

Take the tent *and* lock the truck, huh? Marlow said. Let the Mongolian nigger sleep in a ditch?

Christ, Alex said. Did I really lock it?

You blipped the damn thing as you stormed off.

Jesus, sorry. I don't remember doing that. How'd you find me?

Just followed the swearing.

What?

I could hear you a fucking mile off. Sweet place to camp, by the way.

Alex unzipped and scrambled out. She'd pitched the tent in a round depression high on the ridge. They must have been walking in circles in the night: the view over the bombed out hills was almost identical to the view from the lookout. Except it was pristine with new snow. And it was backwards.

Oh shit, she whispered, dropping to a crouch. They were looking back towards Russia from the opposite side of the valley. They'd stumbled through no man's land, across the border into Mongolia, and camped in a bomb crater.

Bullseye, Marlow said, poking his head from the tent. Blizzard must have grounded the drones.

Alex whistled. How long do you think we've got before they dig out the runways?

You tell me. Could be hours, could be days.

Days? Alex said. She stood and scanned the absurdly blue sky. Nothing. She looked south, into the war-torn interior. You got your pack, right? she asked.

Yeah, Marlow said. Why?

I've got my camera. We've got everything we need.

Tranquillisers, Marlow said. That's what you need.

We can make it to the Protected Area in four or five

days, Alex said. There were villages round there. We film whatever we find, then get out. Let's blow this thing wide open.

Marlow tapped the side of his head. What, this thing? I'll buy you a beer.

Oh, what the hell, Marlow said. Let's get killed.

Down that day and up the next, Alex and Marlow followed the GPS south through snow-bound hills. Cold air burned in their lungs. They wandered charred corridors where drones had come down among the trees. The snapped trunks resembled the pillars of ruined temples, leading to altars of heat-deformed steel.

Further from the border there seemed less wreckage. They began to see snow hares and the precise tracks of foxes. At night wolves called to a brilliant frozen sky.

Three days in, they caught the hiss of resumed drone flights along the border. A squadron of blue-grey fighters slit the sky from east to west. That night they woke to the ground-shaking *crump* of explosives. Alex unzipped the tent. The skyline beyond the trees rippled and burned in a terrifying light show.

The next day they found a road, winding south out of the hills towards the Ghenghis Khan Protected Area, where the fighting had been most fierce. The surface of the road was churned by the tracks of huge vehicles. Alex crouched to take photographs. A flock of crows launched into flight above them.

Marlow looked up. Move it!

They clawed their way up the bank as the gun barrel of a Chinese drone tank swung around the bend.

The monstrous grey-white vehicle ground through the snow at speed. Five more thundered past. Next came a line of drone fuel tankers, then more tanks bringing up the rear. The convoy passed on and was gone.

Alex rolled onto her back and blew out her breath in a long cold plume. Now we're getting serious, she said.

She was halfway to her feet when Marlow dragged her back down. The revs of another tank column filled the valley. Patton tanks: American. One after another the armoured beasts shot past in pursuit. Alex brought her camera to her eye. More supply trucks, more tanks. Then just the reek of diesel and the empty road. Marlow was digging frantically in his pack.

What? Alex said.

Vest, girl. They gonna be blazing.

They waited in fear for the bombardment to start. The seconds slowed into minutes, and the valley's hush grew deep. Then the dusk air burst with the roar of cannons. Alex heard the shriek of falling shells, saw a crackling, strobing light several valleys over. She couldn't hold the camera still enough to get a decent shot.

For the next two days they shadowed the road to

the Protected Area. Every four or five hours a Chinese or American convoy churned its way upstream towards the battle zone. The fighting always began at dusk. Heading towards the fiery horizon felt like madness. As they neared where the villages had been, Marlow grew quiet. Alex had a constant low grinding in her belly, part hunger and part nerves, but she pushed them both on. This was her chance. This was what journalists did.

The forest began to thin. At this lower altitude the snow was mostly gone. On the far side of the ridge was the Protected Area. They tightened their pack straps and slogged up the slope.

From the news footage she'd seen, Alex knew what to expect: a nightmare of razed villages and twisted fuselage. And that was the official version. She knew Hurtz and the army must be hiding bodies, and she would find them. Mongolian men and women lying in the mud, children too, dead and cold. Without make-up or artifice she would turn to the camera and call Hurtz out. She would end the false accounting of Zero Zero Zero.

Alex reached the crest of the ridge, steeled herself, and drew in a breath at what she saw.

A sudden sweeping view of paradise.

Late-afternoon sun lit a valley of open grassland, surrounded on all sides by timbered hills. The road followed the silver windings of a river, then turned into a complex of buildings that might have been a military base or factory. Distant workers moved around a series of small pools. A recovery drone, lights winking in the dusk, came in to land. The breeze carried the steady thump of heavy machinery.

Where's the war? Alex said.

Marlow shrugged, his face caught between confusion and relief.

An American convoy rolled in through the complex gates. Figures moved towards the trucks to unload. Alex raised her camera and filmed a few precious seconds, and as she did, excitement rose through the fog of her exhaustion. Here, surely, was the heart of her film.

Right on dark they approached the nearest gate. There were no guards. They moved cautiously up the raked-pebble drive. There was a sharp series of detonations and an almighty flash. Alex and Marlow threw themselves down.

A salvo of rockets blasted into the sky, arcing up and out in whistling parabolic curves. They drifted high, almost out of sight, and were gone to tiny falling cinders, then exploded in starbursts of red and white and blue.

Fireworks? Marlow said, dazed. We been freaking out 'bout goddamn *fireworks*?

They pulled themselves off the ground. Alex was too confused to reply. Up close she could see the complex was neither army base nor factory. The buildings were elegant slabs of glass, fronted with marble columns after the neoclassical malls of Dubai.

The workers weren't workers, either: they stood round in aggressively cut swimwear, watching the conflagration above. Beyond, American and Chinese army officers played each other at a bizarre mix of volleyball and boxing. Alex and Marlow trudged past in snow fatigues and battered helmets, bent beneath the weight of their packs, capturing it all on film. No one paid them any attention.

From behind, horns blared. Marlow and Alex turned, blinded, and were run off the road by a wedge of golf buggies. Alex glimpsed jowled and whooping Chinese and American generals at the controls. They slammed to a halt beside a newly arrived supply convoy, and joined the mob of officers and arms dealers wrestling cases of champagne from the trucks. Someone dropped a case and the bottles went up like grenades. The air crackled with fireworks and laughter, shouting in a dozen tongues, and a sudden pungent rain from the rockets above. The revellers raised their hands and opened their mouths. Caviar Monday, baby! a voice yelled.

Somewhere nearby a door opened. There was a spill of boozy cheering, of whistles and horns. The chug of machinery crisped into the bass, kick, snare of nineties house. People streamed past towards the music.

Come on, you two! someone shouted. She's starting!

The American woman on the door looked at them hard. She tilted her head to one side, then turned and consulted with a thickset Chinese man. He nodded.

Door prize! the woman yelled.

Door prize? Marlow echoed.

Those giant backpacks! And that starved look, and the zeal in your eyes—that's gold. Congratulations. She handed Marlow an envelope full of drinks tickets. Enjoy.

The corridor opened onto a vast, smoke-filled nightclub styled like a Mongolian village, right down to the dirt floor and roaming goats. One of the goats was being strung up over a fire, its throat cut, and Alex realised the place *was* a Mongolian village; they'd built the club over the top.

Bass pounded from the sound system. Defence contractors shimmied past in aviators and Hawaiian shirts, cameras round their necks. An arms dealer Alex recognised from her documentary chugged his beer to a chant of *Scoop! Scoop! Scoop!* There were half a dozen John Pilger lookalikes, identical in flak jackets and grey wigs.

What's the theme tonight? Alex asked a passing waiter.

The man looked at her, confused. Journalists, he said. You look fine. Maybe a bit over the top, but fine.

Up on the main stage the DJ finished his set, and a karaoke machine was wheeled out. A short brunette clutching a glass of champagne came on to tremendous cheers. She launched into a bizarre rendition of 'Total

Eclipse of the Heart'. Each time her babyish voice crooned the chorus, a wag down the back hollered: Of darkness!

Marlow was watching the singer closely. I'll be damned, he said.

What's wrong? Alex asked.

Look.

Swaying on absurd platform shoes, her familiar face addled with booze, droning into the microphone in a saccharine whisper, was General Hurtz.

Alex felt her fatigue vanish. She dropped her pack and thrust the camera into Marlow's hands. This is it, she said. Don't worry about me. Just get the footage out.

What are you going to do? Marlow asked.

Alex smiled grimly. Interview the shit out of her.

Then she was off, cutting through the crowd like an icebreaker, climbing the stairs to the stage, growing fierce with each stride. The general looked up in confusion. Alex towered over her. She grabbed the microphone and the music abruptly cut.

General Hurtz, she boomed into the silence. What have you done with the war?

The crowd howled with laughter. There were cries of *Scoop! Scoop! Scoop!*

Oh, I get it, Hurtz said. You're being a journalist. Very good. Now take a hike.

I'm serious, Alex said.

Hurtz fumbled in her pocket. She was wearing a

deconstructed general's uniform, dyed gold and reworked to resemble a straitjacket. She found her glasses and put them on, and found Alex staring down at her, eyes steady and fierce beneath the helmet.

You look like you're dressed for a war, Hurtz said.

I heard there was one round here, Alex said. Seen it?

Hurtz took another microphone from its stand. Friends! she cried. I have a report of a missing war. Anyone seen a war round here?

The crowd roared.

We kidnapped it and tortured it! someone shouted.

No, really, Alex said. What the fuck's happened to it?

What does it look like? Hurtz said, raising her champagne flute. We've stolen it.

This time the crowd went wild, screaming and drumming their feet.

But tell me, Hurtz said once the noise died down, didn't you used to be famous?

Alex scowled. Notorious, she said.

That's right! Hurtz said. You're that newsreader who blew up on air. Friends, we have a real-deal journalist in the house—please make her welcome!

Excited cheers filled the club. The crowd pushed in close to get a better look. They seemed to think it was part of the night's entertainment. *Looks just like her*, Alex heard someone say. A group of military police were pushing their way through the tightly packed crowd. Marlow was slouched against a speaker stack to one side, helmet over his eyes, camera held at waist height. The red recording light shone steadily.

So tell me, General Hurtz, Alex said. What is this place?

Hurtz's eyes darted to the back of the club. What do you say, she asked the crowd, playing for time. Shall we tell the journalist our secret?

Yes! they shouted, with such force that Alex saw the general blink.

Well, then, Hurtz said. What is this place? You've heard of hollow government? This is what's inside the hollow.

Right, Alex said, confused. What about the trillion-dollar war? Where's that? Inside the hollow too?

Hurtz smiled. It's amazing what we can do with computers these days.

With *computers*?

One enormous system. See there, above the bar?

Instead of the news, a row of screens showed close-ups of teenagers' faces, staring into the camera with furious concentration. Explosions, instrument controls and Mongolian terrain reflected in their eyes.

Hyper-real three-D, Hurtz said. Everyone plugs in, from the pilots to the media. Apart from the people in this room, everyone thinks they're getting live camera feeds.

Bullshit, Alex said. You can't fake a war.

It's not fake, Hurtz said. It's being fought virtually.

Alex raised her eyebrows.

We are absolutely at war, Hurtz said. Pilots fly missions, patriots crowd the streets. The fighting all happens overseas anyway, so who cares if it's virtual or real?

There were murmurs of assent from the crowd.

If I attacked you, Alex said, you'd care if it was virtual or real.

Precisely, Hurtz replied, warming to her subject. I'd prefer it to be virtual. We all would, when the loss of one life makes so little difference to the cause. War is fundamentally economic. You lose when you run out of resources. The blood and fire is just a distracting spectacle. We've agreed with our Chinese friends to step up the spectacle, and eliminate the real blood and fire. The economic base remains unchanged. Whoever runs out of money first will lose.

But if there's no war, what the hell are you spending the money on?

Billions on the computer systems. Billions on enough real drones to make it plausible.

And the rest?

Profit.

There were whistles and claps from the floor.

Are you fucking serious? Alex said. You must have stolen a trillion dollars.

Hurtz took off her glasses in a decisive gesture Alex recognised from TV. Don't be naïve, Hurtz said. War's a business, same as any other. We deliver it for cheap, the profits are ours to spend. Besides, what's a few air-freighted lobsters when we've saved millions of lives?

Alex felt a surge of rage. You haven't saved lives, she said. It's not real. There are no armies and no fighting. It's fraud, on the most outrageous scale.

Hurtz gave a delighted hoot. No armies and no fighting? she said, turning to the crowd. What do we call that?

Peace! they howled.

Peace? Alex cried. You—

We're not the only ones, Hurtz said. You should watch this year's Nobel Prize announcements.

Peace, Alex started again, is not—

Listen to me, Hurtz said, her voice swelling to fill the room. After the Cold War, Fukuyama said history had ended. He was wrong. The conflicts that drive history forward still happen, and they happen for us, and because of us, but not *to* us. History hasn't ended. It's been outsourced.

But—

Think of all the proxy wars. All the tech we've built to safely fight war at arm's length—air strikes, stealth bombers, cruise missiles. And now we have drones. Hallelujah! We can fight full-scale wars without a single soldier getting out of bed. All we're doing here is taking the next logical step. We've outsourced warfare, in its entirety, to computers.

The assembled staffers, arms dealers and high-ranking officers were quiet now, standing with their faces lifted to

Hurtz. Even the cohort of military police had stopped at the foot of the stage to listen.

Let me ask you a question, Hurtz said. What difference did your famous meltdown make? How many pilots now work from home because of you? How many lives have you saved?

When my film's done—

Your film? What good is a film, against *this*? Hurtz said, sweeping a hand around the enormous militarised nightclub. Against the fact that war's in our blood? The reason people like you fail is because you waste your time asking: how do we eliminate war? The real question is: what kind of war is closest to peace?

Alex turned from the general and crossed to the far side of the stage, trying to clear her head.

There are many types of war, Hurtz continued. And we have the power to choose. How about if this war was physically real? Drone versus drone: would you prefer that? Thousands of lethally armed robots engaged in the annihilation of this country, its environment and people? Costs far beyond the trillion spent so far. Mongolians dead on the ground, right where we stand. Would that make you happy? Would it bring us closer to peace?

Or maybe you'd like us to go back to the old, asymmetrical warfare. Drone versus human: massive lethal force deployed on mere suspicion. Signature strikes on weddings and funerals? Wrong time, wrong place, wrong colour? No? Then let's go further back. We could just have a traditional war. Human versus human: millions sent to the slaughter, millions caught in the crossfire. Cities razed. Unmarked mass graves. How about that?

No? But why stop there? Let's all just meet in a paddock and slaughter each other with sharpened sticks. Or our bare hands. You and me. Right now. Let's scratch and kick and tear each other to bloodied pieces, right here on this stage. Because that's what war was—before it was privatised. Is that what you want? Is that your idea of peace?

Alex turned back to face the general. She'd just worked out how her film would end. She removed her steel helmet, felt its weight in her hand. She felt calm; peaceful, even.

Let me ask you again, Hurtz was saying. In your heart, would you prefer this war was real? Or will you accept our war, and so accept peace? You know this is the better path. Not one person injured. Not one person killed. Say it with me. Us, Them, Civilians—

Us, Them, Civilians, the crowd chanted. Zero, Zero, Zero.

Us, Them, Civilians, Alex said. One, Zero, Zero.

*One*, Zero, Zero? Hurtz said, frowning.

Sorry, Alex said, crossing the stage. I never was any good at math.

# FACEBOOK REDUX

MICHAEL SHOWERS and shaves, then snaps a few self-portraits in the mirror. He lifts his phone high, tilts his head and pouts. *Click.*

He's a substantial man, with ruddy jowls, a small, pleasant mouth and cheerful eyes. At sixty-seven his head is a gleaming dome. Most of his male friends are doing that ridiculous neo-combover thing: a few last pathetic hairs brushed down over one eye, emo-style. He prefers total baldness—chemo-style. *Click.*

Michael stands back and takes a coy full-length shot, half turned to hide his cock. He's in good shape these days. He used to have to watch his weight, with all the dinner parties and long lunches, the breakfasts in bed with Margot. *Click.*

His smile is captured mid-collapse. He deletes the shot. These days he mostly steams a few vegetables. He really has lost a lot of weight. He thinks of it as a small, positive side effect of his wife's death.

In the kitchen there's no sign of Sophie. It's half seven, and she has classes at eight. While Michael waits for coffee, morning images from friends blink up in his retina overlay. He's intrigued, and mildly annoyed, that the system keeps choosing sequences from women his age. There's more from Bernadette. Her dyed black hair is glossy and tousled, and she holds one hand across her breasts. She looks wonderful at seventy, though the effect hasn't been the same since her mastectomy.

These days, he thinks, we're all a bit maimed.

There's a knock at the front door. Michael blinks. Odd—nothing registers in his overlay. He hears Sophie's bedroom door open, then the shower. He carries his coffee down the hall and opens the door.

He can't see anyone there; just a jogger across the street, kids ambling off to school, two gaunt shanty-dwellers having their morning bucket bath on the footpath. Each of them appears in his overlay as a faint swarm of data, visible, available.

Morning!

It's Sophie's friend Eloise, standing on the bottom

step. He stares. She's wearing an emerald headscarf that surrounds her face like a cowl. Is Sophie ready? she asks.

Surprise makes Michael abrupt. No, he says. What's with the scarf?

I've taken the vow. Sophie didn't tell you?

No. Come in.

He stands aside and sips his coffee to hide his distaste. He sees more kids wearing the scarves every day. To him, their cloistered faces look like they have something to hide. He wonders what her parents think. It was one of the few things he and Margot had argued about. He agreed with the papers: privacy led to political unrest. Nonsense, Margot had said. They've got every right to disappear.

So you're just—disconnected? Michael asks Eloise at the kitchen table. He finds it unnerving, talking to someone with zero data presence. It's like sitting across from a small black hole.

We can still access everything, Eloise says. We're just not sending anything out.

And what brought this on? Is it a religious thing?

No, it was History of Privacy. You should hear the lectures. People used to just give it up, for free. There was this thing called Facebook, where you—

*Facebook.* The word comes to him out of a dream.

You mean the website? he says.

Yeah. Have you heard of it?

I used to use it.

Eloise sits forward with a kind of excited repulsion. Really? You were one of them? So did you just give away your—everything?

That's a personal question, he says. He's joking, but she blushes anyway.

Sophie bangs into the kitchen, hair damp from the shower. Are you hassling Lou?

She's hassling me, Michael says. About my time on Facebook.

Sophie looks dismayed. You were on *Facebook*?

I was. Your mother, too. We—

Michael trails off. He's suddenly wide awake. He had completely forgotten: Margot was on Facebook.

Two years on, his natural memory of Margot is as frayed as old rope. He has a wealth of digital captures, but he's exhausting them too. There was one he used to loop, of Margo singing in the shower. He went about his day with the hiss of water and her sweet, off-key high notes ghosting down the hall. Over time it had become background noise: a radio left on in another room.

But Margot was on Facebook. She would have posted videos and photos, decades ago. It's like he's discovered a forgotten chamber of his mind. The thought is exquisite.

Michael realises Sophie has asked him a question. Sorry? he says.

You do own your data, don't you?

Absolutely not, he says. Everything's out in the open.

Why lock yourself away?

Eloise smiles at Sophie. PP, she murmurs. Sophie looks embarrassed.

What's that? Michael says.

You're PP, Eloise says. Post Privacy. We call it Publicly Promiscuous.

He laughs. The wall clock chimes eight.

*Merde*, Sophie says. We're late.

They're halfway down the hall when the thought strikes him.

Hey, girls, he calls. If I'm PP, what are you?

PPP, Eloise says. She flashes a small gold ring over her shoulder. Post Post Privacy. We're saving our data for someone special.


Michael has no appointments in the morning. He calls his secretary. With your permission, he says, I'd like to engage in a little senile leisure time.

He sits at the desk in his study and thinks about Facebook. His retina and cortex are hardwired, like everyone else on his income, and the results come up in his overlay. There's a wealth of historical analysis and old news items. Then he finds what he's looking for. In a grey zone of southern Russia's deep web, buried in the sediment of an archival server, is a copy of the Facebook data. A fossilised social network.

He's not expecting much when his system attempts to connect, but a moment later, there it is: the homepage. It's surprisingly familiar, right down to the precise shade of blue. At the top is a link: *Recover your profile*.

Not bloody likely, he says aloud. It's been forty-odd years. But he follows the link, skips the privacy statement and fills in a form. His overlay shows ancient code routines waking from sleep on the host server. Obsolete analytics grasp at new filaments of data. There's another procedure too, shimmering just below the intelligible horizon, that his own system does not recognise.

While he waits, Michael crosses to the window. Another mainland family is building a tarpaulin shanty on the nature strip. The young father waves; he's not too badly burned. Michael would have been about that age when social media took over his life. Twenty-three? Twenty-three and full of love, and full of himself. He remembers Margot teasing him about wasting his life self-promoting on Facebook. So much so that he deleted the thing...Shit. They both did. It felt like a spiritual breakthrough at the time. They deleted their profiles, went to Thailand, got married, got on with their lives, and now she's dead.

Michael's in the kitchen, trying to summon enthusiasm for work, when it blinks up in his overlay. *Profile reactivated. Welcome back.*

His profile picture stares at him across the decades. His head is shaved, cocked to one side, lit with an insolent grin. It's eerily similar to the picture he snapped this morning. He runs a hand over the wearied flesh of his face. What skin—what a pup!

Beneath his photo is a random-seeming list of things he'd claimed to like. Cormac McCarthy. Someone called Seamus Heaney. *The Wire*. It seems so archaic—that you would tell a system what you liked, rather than trusting it to tell you. There is an invitation to something called a Permablitzkrieg, and one to a Climate Action Rally, back when they thought they stood a chance. He didn't want to think about it then, and he doesn't want to think about it now. He scrolls down.

His heart lurches. There's something from Margot.

It's a photo, too small to properly make out, but she looks to be pulling a face. Below, it says: *This content has been removed by the user.*

Michael clicks through to her profile. That same line is repeated, time and again. He clicks through messages, events and comments, drumming his fingers in irritation. The same fuzzy avatar makes the same taunting declaration. It's as if Margot removed herself to spite him.

He scrolls through photos, hoping to glimpse her in other people's shots, and before long he's distracted. Long-dead friends beam their vitality through the years. They're in and out of clubs, crammed in the back of cars, camped among valleys of tangled bush. He lingers over a shot of himself diving off the side of a boat at dawn. He is reaching down through the bright and liquid air, an instant before the surface is broken. He can't find a single person crying, or angry. Everyone seems brand new.

Halfway down the page, Michael finds a sequence from a woman with an expressive, intelligent mouth and smoky eyes. It only takes a second to remember who she is.

June-Mee! he says aloud.

Michael clicks through to her profile. There's a new entry at the top of the page, exactly the same as his own.

*Profile reactivated. Welcome back.*

Michael gradually becomes conscious of a rattling from the air purifier on the wall. He stretches over and gives it a whack that makes his hand sting. He can't believe he's found someone else on the network.

He loses an hour trawling through old photos. She's lazing on a beach in Greece, hiking in the Yellow Mountains out past Shanghai. The images stir something in him. Curiosity, and nostalgia.

They'd met at a party. He'd walked into the crowded bathroom and she was reclined in the bathtub, laughing among the ice and beer, reciting some speech she was studying. Their eyes had met.

Free at last, she cried. Free at last!

On a whim, he sends her a message.

Later, he is propped in bed reading, still carefully

on his own side of the bed, when a reply comes through.

*Michael, what a surprise! Are you well?*

He gives a wriggle of delight and kicks off the sheets. The chatter in his overlay is immediate and positive: eighty-eight per cent of his friends are intrigued. Sophie, studying in her room, sends a *WTF*. She turns up her music, and it seeps through their shared wall.

Michael starts each day searching for traces of Margot, and ends up chatting with June-Mee. He finds her quick and funny. It seems she's the only other living person on Facebook, and he likes the irony: from a billion people down to two. She hints at a simple, affluent life. They both live in the leafy suburbs of Tasmania's Greater Melbourne, and he gets the feeling she's recently divorced. He doesn't ask for details. He mentions Margot's death and Sophie's presence, in passing. They talk as if they're still twenty-one.

June-Mee recalls a night when they took ecstasy in his bedroom, then cried with laughter through a dinner with scandalised friends. She had a boyfriend who lived interstate. He recalls the sexual tension of their nights out, a gaunt stranger in a club asking if they were lovers. They weren't—but if he's honest, he wishes they had been.

Michael wakes a few days later with a good restlessness in him. He catches Sophie at the breakfast table. Her hair is getting long, and she's taken to wearing it pulled across her face. She ignores his questions about school. She won't be drawn on the History of Privacy. He stops trying to sidle up to the conversation.

I discovered an old friend on Facebook, he says.

I know, she says. It's creepy. Don't you think it's weird how she just found you?

I found her. June-Mee is a lovely woman. She makes me feel—

Just don't, she says. It's private.

It's not private, he says, amused. I want to share it with you.

Sophie stares into her coffee mug. You've already shared it with anyone who'll listen.

It's worth sharing.

You think brushing your teeth is worth sharing. Eloise says you make your life cheap by just giving it away.

That's ridiculous, he says. What does it cost you to be open about your life?

It costs—something.

Rubbish. It costs to be private. Do you have any idea how much Eloise's parents will be spending to let her turn off her—

He catches himself.

Sorry, he says. Look, do you think this is disrespectful

to your mother? To have dinner with June-Mee?

Maybe, Sophie says. Yes. And to you. Couldn't you just do something for yourself?

You mean, do something private? he says.

Yes.

Turn everything off?

Would you?

Well, Michael says. I guess.


Michael showers and shaves, and slips into his old dinner jacket. He lifts his phone. *Click*.

The jacket is far too big. More than that, it reminds him overwhelmingly of Margot. The feeling of buttoning it up in the mirror, the tang of aftershave, the anticipation of good food: he is dragged so sharply back to their shared life that he is forced to leave the jacket on the bed.

On the way into town his overlay briefly takes over the driving. The doors lock and the car cuts west, through the vast shadowed slums of New Brunswick to a boutique overlooking the city's western firebreak. The staff have a simple but expensive blazer picked out when he arrives, precisely to his taste and cut. He knows he doesn't need to check it in the mirror.

Outside the restaurant Michael stops to turn off his phone. It's a symbolic act, because most of the hardware is carried under his skin. But he mutes it all, and one by one the chattering streams of data that have accompanied his adult life fade away. His overlay is gone. The streetscape and the passing crowds flatten into surface and light.

Beside the restaurant door there is a man with his hand out, begging. The faint swarm of data around him winks out, and Michael finds himself staring into the man's face. Two bloodshot blue eyes, without lids, gaze back at him from a mask of flesh so badly burned it wears no recognisable human expression. Air sucks and blows from two small holes. Michael fumbles a note into the man's hand, and pushes open the restaurant door.

There are two women sitting by themselves, both with their backs to him. As he approaches the first he sees straight away that she is too young. Her hair spills long and dark down her back. He passes the table and fixes his attention on the next woman, sitting alone with a book and a glass of wine. His pulse quickens.

A voice calls to him from behind. Michael?

He turns. It *is* June-Mee sitting at the first table. She rises in greeting and a shock goes through him. She is twenty-three or twenty-four. Thirty at most. Her skin, beneath the lightest dusting of make-up, is flawless. When she smiles, he sees the same strong teeth that bit his bottom lip when they kissed on his doorstep, that one and only time.

Michael, she says again. It's me. June-Mee.

Hello, he says. You look—lovely.

She searches his face, affectionate and curious. How are you? she says.

I'm good, he says. I'm great. And you?

They dive into conversation. Michael talks and laughs, but he's on autopilot. His mind grasps for clarification. He turns to his overlay and the datasphere and his friends, but they're gone. Soup comes, he eats it, the waiter removes the bowls. He tastes none of it. Is this her daughter? Has she had surgery? It can't be her, and yet it is, unmistakeably, the woman he knew some forty years ago. The way she talks, excited and playful and sharp, and her ready laugh, even the way her elbows tuck to her sides when she walks to the bathroom: it's her.

When she returns he fumbles towards the question. So, what have you been doing for the last forty years? How come you look so—good?

You remember I went to France? June-Mee says. I started a fashion label, skirts made from vintage men's suits. Like the one I wore to—

The conversation swings back to the past and they're off again, reminiscing and laughing. The next time he tries, she turns the conversation to him. He finds himself talking about Sophie.

She insisted I meet you in private, he says. I was going to turn up in a green headscarf.

He talks about his fears, his hopes. It floods out of him. June-Mee asks perceptive questions, and follows his answers, even when he wanders into the dull maze of his professional life. She laughs at his tales of how he avoided the horrors of the thirties, and reaches across to cuff him when he grows cheeky with wine. He avoids talking about Margot.

After the dessert plates are cleared, and the two of them are standing out in the street, wrapped in their coats with the taste of coffee on their lips, while Michael is summoning the courage to ask her, once and for all, what's going on, he realises he can't handle this by himself.

He's desperate for clarification. But it's more than that: he has to share this feeling. It means nothing if he keeps it to himself. A maimed beggar cannot be his only witness. Michael switches everything on, and as the real world comes swarming in, June-Mee kisses him on the mouth.

Goodbye, Michael.

Her lips are soft and yet firm. As different from his own clumsy lips as can be. He can't believe how good it feels. It's been decades since he's had a kiss like this. June-Mee doesn't have to reach up like Margot did. She simply presses into him, her body lithe against the swell of his belly. As the moment—its image, its imprint, its strange reality—flows outwards through the datasphere, he feels joy blooming inside him, ruthless and swift.

Goodbye, Michael.

She bites his bottom lip, and is gone.

Michael showers, long and vague beneath the scalding water. He doesn't bother shaving. A hangover beats on his skull. He raises his phone and snaps off the morning's shots. *Click.*

It's all there in his face. Guilt hangs in the shadows under his eyes. But there's more: the conflicted beginnings of a smile. He needs coffee. Sophie will already be at school. He makes his way slowly down the hall in just his towel.

Sophie is waiting for him in the kitchen. The first thing he sees is the emerald headscarf pulled low over her brow. He scans her data in a panic. Total blackout. She looks furious.

Are you going to pay? she says.

What? What are you doing wearing—

You haven't even looked at it, have you? Here.

She blinks, and his overlay fills with Cyrillic characters. He dimly remembers seeing it when he woke.

What's that?

That's the bill, she says.

For what?

You went on a date with a twenty-four-year-old woman from your past, she says.

I don't understand, he says.

No shit. Did she know exactly what you liked?

Michael nods.

Did she have an unbelievable memory?

I guess.

She was pretty much perfect, right?

Well—

And you don't own your own data?

I told you, Michael says. Of course not.

See, that's how they do it! After you shared your disgusting little moment with the world, I looked it up.

Michael sits at the table. The towel rides up around his thighs. He tugs it down. You're going to have to spell this out, he says.

You've let them log everything you've ever done, she says. They know what you've watched and bought and clicked. They even know what porn you like—they use that too. It's in the fine print when you reactivate your Facebook account. You're liable for premium services.

She's not real? he says feebly.

She's a *premium service*, Dad. They used to send emails from Natalya in Russia, wanting to meet for a good time. This is just the latest version of the scam. Wait, what's the woman's name again?

June-Mee, he says. June-Mee Kim.

Sophie blinks, accessing her own data. Hang on, she says. Yes, here. Did you even check outside Facebook? Jesus, she died twenty-five years ago.

She sees his expression, and the righteousness fades from her face.

Dad, she says. I know you've been lonely. But so do

they; they know how you're feeling better than you do. It's total manipulation.

They've built this—woman—out of everything I've ever said and done?

Pretty much.

Michael is quiet for a long time. And you've taken the vow? he says.

Sophie places her hand on the table, and he sees the small gold ring. She tilts her chin defiantly. Yes, she says. Eloise came over last night.

He tries her data stream one more time. Nothing. She's beyond him now, encrypted to hell. He thinks of Margot—their life, their shared history—and how she is beyond him too.

Then he thinks of June-Mee, and the taste of her lips, and how June-Mee is right here. Michael looks at the bill. He can afford it.

# HOW MUCH COURAGE

EUCHIE LOOKED out her bedroom window to the mudflats and the bay. At the heads, one last lazy swirl of gulls was settling into the cliffs for the night. Beyond was just the sun-strafed bloom of monsoon clouds and a wedge of empty sea.

The volunteer gun emplacement winked red atop the narrows. The eighty-pounder swivelled to the west and shrugged, then came the window-rattling *thump* and flash.

Euchie stripped off her shorts and singlet. She chose a floral sundress with straps across her dark tanned back. Next she pulled on a pair of hand-me-down stockings from her mum. In this heat the nylon was a delicious, adult suffocation. They'd gone saggy at the knees, but it wasn't like any boy would be getting a look. They were all away on militia training until forever.

She smiled at herself in the mirror, and kept smiling till it looked natural. She went down the stairs. It was six o'clock. Her mum would be cleaning the gun.

Fran had the citizen's-issue Glock laid out in pieces on the kitchen table. She worked the cleaning rod into the barrel. It wasn't that she hated night shifts. Everyone had to do their bit, and it was mostly peaceful up there at the old *pa* site, watching the horizon for boats. She just didn't like leaving Euchie to her own devices for so long. She dropped oil into the trigger assembly and snapped the magazine into place. She looked up as Euchie came down the stairs.

Look at you! she cried. What a beauty. Where to tonight?

The esplanade, Euchie said. We heard there might be boats in the bay. Maybe a beach party.

Ha ha, Fran said. She handed Euchie the gun. Give them my best. Remember, shoot your friends first, then yourself.

I know, Mum.

I'd do it myself if I didn't have to work.

Ha ha back, Euchie said. What's your shift?

On the radar till four.

Fran crossed to the door. As she bent to lace her boots she noticed Euchie's legs. Her daughter had shot up like a baby giraffe in the last year but the stockings, with their ridiculous ballooning kneecaps, made her seem more girlish than ever. Fran forced herself to smile. Make sure you're home by nine, she said. Text me when you get in.

Yes, Mum. Love you.

Love you too. Bye.

On the back porch the dog lay sprawled in the heat. Fran knelt at the retriever's flank and ran a hand beneath her greying muzzle.

Don't you worry, darling, Fran murmured. I'd shoot you too.

Euchie did her make-up. She carved herself a new red mouth and blackened her eyes. She hung forbidden pirate hoops from her ears. She checked her phone and put the Glock in her handbag, then walked to the beach, singing as she went. Her voice carried thin and high in the breeze.

> *Mother, oh mother*
> *You've got that look again*
> *Daughter, oh daughter*
> *Keep that face hidden.*

The sea mouthed and suckled in the mangroves. There were no cars. The houses littering the hill were dark, and the tiny strip of shops across the river stood dark as well.

At the esplanade Marama and Allie were waiting by the boat ramp. They were two skinny girls in matching boob tubes. Marama was Euchie's best friend. Allie was a bitch, but not all the time.

How's the you-know-what? Marama asked.

Euchie shrugged. Lost a morning yesterday, but today was okay. Mum still doesn't know.

I had a near thing at the chemist, Marama said. Got out in time, but the lady behind the counter watched me all the way up the street.

Paranoid cow, Allie said.

She's not paranoid, Euchie said. Everyone knows it's here.

Yeah, Allie said, but who's going to admit it?

The three of them sat among the scorched timbers littering the beach. They smoked monsoon-damp cigarettes, and gossiped as the sun sank below the hills that ringed the town.

You ever wonder where it really came from? Euchie said.

Those coastguard guys that boarded the first boats, Allie said. Before they knew what it was. Gave it to their kids, then it got into the schools.

I know that, Euchie said. But that was down south, and they're all quarantined. You ever see a boat land round here?

They had a dozen past the battery at Ahipara, Allie said.

Yeah, and they shot them all on the beach. But it's everywhere now.

So?

I reckon it was already here.

Maybe a bit, Allie said, a frown in her voice. But it didn't make whole cities shut down.

Euchie shrugged. It was hard to argue with that.

Out past the headlands, a spotter drone buzzed overhead.


They were talking about boys when the truck pulled in. For a moment the waves were lit, curling and dropping in a shaggy spray, and then the headlights snapped off. Euchie heard deep voices and the clink of bottles.

Who's that? Marama said, hitching up her boob tube.

Euchie stood and peered into the near dark. A phone chimed and its screen blinked on. She saw a man in profile, the sharp peak of his cap.

Militia, Euchie said.

What the hell? Allie said. They shouldn't be here. Must be something big.

Who's there? a voice called. Identify yourselves.

A torch raked the sand, then fixed upon the three squinting girls.

Well, *hello*, a man's voice said. Mind if we join you?

Dunno if we should, came a deeper voice.

Chill, bro, the first man said. His voice was light and smooth as driftwood. It'll be fine.

Come on, fellas, Euchie called. Don't be shy.

The five men carried their cartons of beer down to the beach. It was hard to tell them apart in the dark. The smooth voice was Sean and the deep voice was Nessi. They had city accents: young men from the suburbs come north to test their nerve. They settled into the sand around the girls.

What are you all doing here? Euchie asked.

Strictly classified, said the one called Sean.

Whatever, Euchie replied. Are there going to be more mass arrivals?

When the next boats arrive, Sean intoned in the voice from the TV, the citizen militias will blah blah blah.

One of the other men did the chant: *We're armed! And willing! And read-dy to fight!*

Nah, bro, another said. Armed and willing and ready to *fuck*.

There was snorted laughter, and the crack and foam of beers.

Anyway, who cares about arrivals, came Nessi's deep voice. When's the last time a boat got past the batteries? The militia's a waste of fucking time.

True that, someone said. The militia should be wasted and fucking—all the time.

The men lapsed back into thin laughter. They hadn't

answered Euchie's question. They drank hard and talked mostly among themselves.

Off to the north the sky lit up, and a fraction later the *thump* of the big gun pounded through them. One of the militiamen started to weep.

Euchie sat up sharply. Hey, she said. Is he—?

Fuck, Sean said. Get him out of here.

Two figures rose and dragged the third sobbing down the beach.

*I won't, you can't make me*, he ranted.

Might as well tell them, bro, Nessi said. If we're gonna expose them.

Expose us to what? Marama asked in a small voice.

The two men stayed quiet.

You've got it, haven't you, Euchie said. You're all infected.

The churn of waves rushed in to fill the silence, then fled back out. Euchie knew she should keep her mouth shut. But she felt sorry for the men.

Us too, she said softly. We got it too.

The men exhaled, and Euchie felt a dangerous intimacy close around them all.

We couldn't hide it any longer, Nessi said. We stole a truck and just bailed, before the sergeant found out.

How bad? Euchie asked.

Bad enough. Some of us are still holding up, but Jem's done.

Down the beach the man called Jem was silhouetted faintly against the breakers, catatonic. Euchie had never seen someone that far gone.

What about you? Sean asked.

We're okay, for now, Euchie said. Our families don't know. What are you going to do?

Dunno, Sean said. Maybe try to get home.

Auckland?

Yeah.

It looks pretty bad on the news.

It's worse, Sean said. It's like *this*.

Euchie felt a sharp horse bite on her knee. She squealed and lunged across the sand, laughing and hitting, and he grabbed and held her hands.

Fran sat at the radar console, fanning herself with the volunteer roster. The door to the gun emplacement stood open in the heat. Her shift partner was Jessica Davis, a retired judge who lived on the other side of the bay.

And how old's your Euchie's now? Jessica was saying.

She's—hang on, Fran said. Got one here. Are you ready?

All right, Jessica said. Go ahead.

Fran read the co-ordinate string off the radar. Jessica punched the details into the targeting computer, one finger at a time. Fran saw a faint gleam through the window as the big gun rotated.

Mind your ears now, Jessica said. The two women slipped on earmuffs, and Jessica opened the firing control panel and hit the button. The gun bucked. Fran felt the pressure wave punch through her chest, and a blast of scorched air blew into the room. The radar blip disappeared. She removed her earmuffs.

—were saying, Jessica said. Your Euchie's how old now?

Fifteen, Fran said.

Hard at that age. They think they're grown up but they're just kids, really. She's still got the world ahead of her.

Still got sadness ahead of her, Fran said, then wished she hadn't. Jessica was looking at her.

What kind of sadness? Jessica asked.

The women's eyes met, and Fran had to look away.

You mean ordinary sadness, Jessica said gently.

Yes, Fran said. Ordinary sadness. Getting her heart broken by boys.

Jessica laughed. That's the cruel, cruel world, my dear. No one can save their kids from that.

Fran smiled and nodded at the gun. Isn't that what we're trying to do?

Jessica laughed even louder. I suppose so. She rose and shuffled out the door to reload. Back soon.

Make it quick, please, Fran called. There's a flotilla coming in from the north-west.

She crossed to the night-vision scope at the window. Beyond the raised earthen lip of the old *pa* fortifications, the flat black sea turned spectral blue. She could see the boats riding in on the tide like a pod of rusted whales. That was a lot of sadness on the way.

She was turning back to the radar when two short, sharp cracks pierced the air.

Small-arms fire. Behind her. From the town.

Jessica's voice. What on earth was—

*Thump.*

The Ahipara battery opening up along the coast.

Then a terrible scraping crash from down in the bay, and a rising wail that turned to screams.

Fran's thoughts fled to Euchie, there on the beach. She swept the scope over the town. Some kind of metal craft pulled up on the sand. People moving. The scope flagged weapons, blinking and blinking in red.

Oh, god, Fran moaned.

Jessica was at her side. What is it?

Something got through. Beached at the esplanade. Gunfire.

Fran moved to the console and took the radio with shaking hands. She'd been expecting this day. Expecting it for years.

All stations, this is battery Tasman-Six-Twenty. Code One. Entry with force, shots fired—

She dropped the radio. She could feel the sadness

rising in herself. There wasn't long.

I'm going, she said. Euchie's down there. I told her to—

You can't go, Jessica said. There's more coming. I can't operate this by myself.

I have to. I couldn't bear it if—

No! Jessica grasped at her arm.

Fran pulled away, and the woman's distinguished face caved in with grief. So, her too.

Fran took a torch and ran.


Sean kept pulling Euchie into his lap. She didn't mind. It was good there in the snug of him, drinking his beer with her head against his chest. It was too dark to see his face, but he had an intoxicating musky reek.

They would totally take over, one of the militiamen was saying. There are a shitload more of them than us.

And they're different from us, another said. Even their accents. They're so fucked up you'd never understand a word.

I don't know, Marama said cautiously. Are they really that different?

Yes, Allie said. They're all infected. I heard you get it just seeing their faces.

They reckon it's in the tears, Nessi said. They told us in training.

So how'd we all get it, then? Euchie said. It's not like we've been drinking their tears.

I have, Sean said. Six pack a day.

You must be real sad, Euchie said.

I'm the saddest mofo in the country.

The others laughed, but Euchie leaned back into him. What's it like, for you? she murmured.

I dunno, Sean said uncomfortably.

You can tell me.

Sean was quiet. It's like…you're filling up with water. Or something's growing inside you. It's dumb.

The others were talking about tear contamination. Euchie tilted her head, and could just make out the line of Sean's jaw against the stars. Like there's something growing? she said.

Yeah.

Same.

For real? Like how?

She reached back and hooked an arm awkwardly round his neck. Don't laugh, she said, but it's like—the bush at night. It goes forever, in all directions. Only they're not normal trees. They're black with black flowers, and they're growing like they're in fast-forward. That's the sadness.

Hmm, Sean said, and Euchie felt the soft vibration through his chest.

And there are these machines, like harvesters, you

know? Only tiny. They're just these little lights moving in the dark, trying to harvest the sadness and keep it at bay. But they can't keep up—

Euchie tailed off, feeling stupid.

And up it comes, Sean said. I know. His arm encircled her and pulled her close.

Euchie closed her eyes.

After a few minutes Sean shifted slightly, and his hand grazed her breast. She thought it was an accident. It happened again.

I heard this helps, he whispered.

With what?

The sadness.

His hand slid rough and warm down the front of her dress, searching out a nipple, and she was flooded with queasy, annihilating heat. She giggled to cover her shock. A moment later his other hand lighted on her thigh, just above the sagging knee of her stockings. She jerked herself into a sitting position, Sean's hand tearing a strap on her dress, and the impulse carried her all the way to her feet. She felt riotous.

What's wrong? Sean said.

Euchie looked past the surf to the open water of the bay. She said the first thing that came into her head. There's a boat.

Huh? Sean said. What?

That's huge, she said, her voice growing firm. Is

that one of ours?

What are you talking about?

There's a boat in the bay.

The bodies sprawled in the sand around her began to stir.

Where? Nessi said.

There. She pointed roughly towards the heads. Marama, can you see it?

Um—

She gave Marama a kick.

Oh, wait, Marama said. There. Holy shit.

It hasn't got any lights on, Euchie said. I don't reckon that's one of ours.

They were all on their feet now.

I can't see it, Nessi said. My eyesight's shit. Where?

Right there, Euchie said. Damn. How'd that get past the battery?

They stood straining their eyes for so long that Euchie could almost imagine a boat, ghosting on the tide with its engines cut.

Wait, Sean said. I see it. I think.

Euchie felt Marama squeeze her hand. She stifled a giggle.

Where? Nessi said.

There, bro, Sean said. I can see something. Right there. Oh, shit.

Wait, Nessi said. Me too. There. I see it too.

Fuck, Sean said. What do we do? Does that mean we—

*Thump.* The coastal battery roared out across the water.

Christ, Nessi said, suddenly shaky. We have to…you know. There's guns in the truck.

Euchie heard a faint flumping sound behind her. Another of the militiamen dropped into the sand and began to sob. There was a rushing sound, and then a splash as Nessi hurled his bottle into the surf.

Fuck it all, he said. This is what we trained for. Let's go. He stumbled up the beach.

Euchie felt hands on her shoulders. It was Sean, close to tears.

If we don't return, he said, farewell.

You'll be okay, Euchie said.

They might have guns.

Guns?

If we survive, I'll come back for you.

His beery breath was on her face and then his mouth was stuck to hers, his tongue was her tongue, and she was brimming with laughter. She choked it off, and it sounded like a sob.

When the men were in the truck, weaving up the esplanade with their headlights off, Euchie took the gun from her bag. She stepped away from Marama and Allie and trained it out to sea. She grinned.

Block your ears, guys.

She pulled the trigger. Twice.

Flame lit the beach from end to end, and the prone shape of Jem was there in the muzzle flash, weeping on the tide line. Sound flooded back with Allie's and Marama's screams. Euchie turned to see the truck veer from the road. The dark mass leaned into space, then tipped and rolled down the bank with a grinding smash.

She put a hand to her mouth and gave a fearful, excited squeal. There were shouts from the truck. An incoherent moaning. Allie was yelling at her. Euchie thrust the pistol into her handbag and bolted down the beach.

When she reached the truck she could just make out the men huddled beside its metal carcass. One was curled in a ball. Most of them were weeping.

Are you okay? Euchie said.

Jesus, Nessi said. Jesus. They opened fire. We're hit. Sean's hurt.

Oh no—

Guilt splashed through her. She dug a lighter from her bag. The darkness flared into a ring of scared and raw-scrubbed faces. They were just boys, barely older than her. Sean's forehead was oily with blood.

Put that out, Nessi hissed. We're sitting ducks.

Euchie swallowed. She had to tell them. There's no boat, she said.

What?

There's no boat. It was me.

Shut up. Listen.

There's no—

*Shh!*

A thin moon had emerged above the headlands, and the curve of the bay stretched away in silver and blue. The faint red light from the gun emplacement glimmered across the waves. Sean whimpered quietly. From down the coast came the thundering of the Ahipara battery.

Then Euchie heard it: a gentle splashing, somewhere just beyond the shore. Waves against a hull. A soft chorus of weeping, and faint voices, accents sharp as knives. It was impossible—she'd made it up.

Christ, Nessi said. They're coming in. We have to get away from the water. Help me.

They dragged Sean up the bank, crying, slipping in loose sand. The other strap on Euchie's sundress snapped. The night licked at her skin. It was so hot, the monsoon close to breaking.

There was movement ahead.

Euchie!

She looked up. Mum, she said, and the sadness took her away.

It was everything Fran feared. She could see the shadowed form of a landing craft on the beach. Men were dragging Euchie up the bank, her dress torn, flesh exposed. The men were weeping with abandon: infected, all of them.

Fran called Euchie's name, and the strength seemed to go out of her daughter. Her legs buckled and she dropped to the sand, her handbag spilling open. Below on the beach the battered prow of another boat crunched ashore. It was too late. The invasion had come.

Fran stumbled down the sandbank. The men ignored her, they were so far gone. She enfolded Euchie's thin shoulders with one arm, and with her free hand rummaged inside the handbag lying on the sand.

She thought about what she had to do and a wail broke from her, and the sound brought forth Euchie's own keening. Their voices wove a song above the beach, soaring and falling, an echo of the *karanga* that sang ashore the first boats, centuries before.

The new arrivals began to drop over the side of their craft into the shallows. Their sobbing carried on the breeze, a terrible chattering grief, scorched and dry. Ghosts of their parched cities across the Tasman. A sunburnt continent, abandoned.

Fran's fingers closed around the gun. It glowed warm and solid in her hand. She looked at the men, and at her daughter, and wondered how much courage she had inside herself. How much courage, and how much love.

# THE CULLER

HE WATCHES the moon lifting huge and pale behind the cut-glass teeth of the Spencer Mountains. The changing light is a miracle. Colour leaches from the midwinter valley, and the ridgelines fold in black like velvet.

There's something else, something he can't quite grasp. Not long ago he would have dropped hard on his belly, safety off, rifle to shoulder. But he's getting better. When the spike of panic goes in he simply stops, breath curling out of him, trying to home in on the feeling.

The air is cold and still. His eyes drift down, from the mountains to the snow-crushed forest and the tumbling river with its mossy bouldered flanks. Mist is ghosting in above the water. In the half-light there's no movement. Nothing.

He's about to move off when it comes again. Not a smell, but the memory of a smell. Smoke. The war is twenty years past but his instinct is good. People.

When he comes across the grassy flats of the Waiheke he sees the moon high above the blue bulk of Mount Ajax, and below, candles burning in the window of the hut. The structure is an ancient pile of rough-hewn logs so ripe with moss it looks to have grown from the earth. He uses it because no one else does. But thirty feet out he gets a hot salty gust of bacon, and voices, smoky and rich—American. He's so tired that the sounds and smells have become one and the same.

He approaches downwind and out of sight, rifle automatically against his far flank so it won't catch the moonlight. At the hut he leans to the fogged glass. There are young fit men ranged around the hearth, sprawled on the sacking bunks. By the fire a man with sandy hair holds a silver tube that looks like toothpaste. He squeezes the contents into his mouth and sluices them around. The others laugh. He swallows, throws the tube in the fire and grins. His voice comes clear through the cracks in the walls.

Okay, you bastards. Now gimme some bacon.

There's a man at the fire holding a frying pan. Uh-uh, he says. No bacon where you're headed.

The culler pulls back from the window. His instinct is to keep moving. But it's six hours to the next hut and he's already exhausted. And he's not one for curiosity but there it is, tugging at him like some old, half-forgotten cruelty. It's too cold and remote for trampers. If they were hunters there'd be rifles outside the door. He watches embers sweep from the chimney into the brilliant night sky. Easy, he tells himself. They're only people.

He doubles back, unloads his rifle and removes the bolt, then crosses the frozen ground in full view, whistling the first few bars of 'The Star-Spangled Banner'. He learned them from a GI in the back of a camion out of Cassino. Eighteen hours jolting, and them all too ruined to say a word except for this sack of a man with a big slow laugh, patriotic for sure but none too bright. Only knew those first heroic bars. Whistled them over and over like an idiot bird.

*O say can you see—*

He's halfway to the hut when the wire latch opens. Light fans the ground.

Hey there! a silhouette calls. It looks like the man with sandy hair.

Gidday, the culler says. His voice sounds like a rusted gate.

Come on in, zero-one-niner. Bet you weren't expecting us.

Can't say I was.

Well, the fire's on. Come and get warm.

The hut is ripe with bacon and sweat. There are six men in all, half his age, focused and lean. It occurs to him that they might be soldiers. There's a chorus of greeting, all *hey* and *howdy*. He leans his rifle in the corner and crosses the room with eyes down. He can feel their gaze, and it takes all his concentration to feign calm.

There's no one on his bunk, but someone's draped a kind of heavy-duty helmeted suit across it. For a moment he stands and stares. He's never seen anything like it.

Sorry, pal. I'll get that. The sandy-haired man heaves the suit onto the top bunk. There ya go. He turns and extends a hand. I'm Neil.

The man has a galaxy of freckles across his nose and cheeks. His eyes are a hopeful blue. Face to face with another man, the culler is suddenly too aware of himself: the bloodied deer tails tied to his pack, his filthy beard, cracked nails and hard hands. He lowers himself abruptly onto his bunk, leaving the man's offering hanging in space.

Good day? Neil asks, undeterred.

I've had better, he says, busy with the straps on his pack. He pulls out a good-sized haunch, cut from a young spiker he'd hit clean through the neck a good half-mile out. He can still make a shot like that out here, away from the drink. He unwraps the fresh meat, and there are whistles and claps.

Look at that. Beautiful.

There ya go, Neil. You don't like the food up there, take a rifle and shoot your own.

The culler takes the haunch and lays it on the bench to start cutting steaks. He risks a glance around. The men's packs are square and hard-looking. Leaned beside the fireplace is a huge American flag, and there's a metal contraption beside him on the bench that might be a camera. Perhaps they're making a movie.

Hunter like you must know the area well.

This from the man tending the frying pan. He seems to be in charge. He's older than the others; just as fit, but thickening round the waist.

Culler, he says.

Excuse me?

Culler. Hunter does it for laughs. Parks Board pays me per tail.

The man is studying his army-issue rifle leaned in the corner. Where'd you learn to shoot, he asks. The war?

Yeah, the culler says, though he's lying. It wasn't shooting the war taught him. He pulls his frying pan from under the bench and the men make room around the fire. He pushes the pan down into the coals. He can't keep his curiosity in.

What are you doing out here? he asks, and wishes he hadn't. The men's sudden quiet is intimidating. He has broken cover, feels himself about to draw fire.

We're scientists, Neil says.

The culler stares at him. Neil doesn't quite meet his eye.

We're with the National Alpine Sciences Association, the older man says. His voice is clear and precise. In for a fortnight's field testing in remote environments, and this here is about the remotest environment on earth.

The culler's heard that sort of thing before. *Field testing.* None of your damn business, more like. He drops a steak into the pan with a squelching hiss. You using this hut as a base? he asks.

The man takes his meaning. Just passing through, he says, turning the bacon in his own pan. Leave you to it. We're heading to Falling Mountain. Know it?

The culler nods.

What's up there?

Rocks.

Rocks?

Mountain came down in a quake. It's like the moon up there.

That right? the man says. He pulls his pan from the fire. Say, you want some bacon?

The culler grunts a negative, but something in his face gives him away. The man has already flipped six fat rashers onto a tin plate and added a slab of bread.

Here, the man says.

He can't refuse. After weeks of venison and damper it smells like heaven. He feels them watching him eat, crabbed over the plate, piling the slick and salty food into his tired body. He has to force himself to slow down.

Neil holds out a plate of his own. C'mon now. My turn?

Focus, the older man says. Have another tube. Right now you're a hundred thousand miles from any such bacon.

Neil doesn't argue. He takes another silver tube from his pack and sucks it down.

What's that? the culler asks.

Food, Neil says. Weighs nothing, and good for you too. Pity it tastes like hell. Here. He tosses a tube across the room.

The culler catches it, and squeezes a little paste onto one calloused finger. He touches it to his tongue. Peanut butter and something else, meaty and rich. Not too bad, he says. Lighter than potatoes.

I bet the Russians take potatoes, someone says.

Yeah, another says. Spudnik.

The hut fills with laughter. The culler doesn't get the joke, but he senses it is not at his expense. The bacon has calmed his hunger. He finds himself cutting his steak into chunks. He offers the plate around and five of them take a slice. Neil ruefully shakes his head.

Twenty-one hundred hours, the older man says. Fifteen to turn-in.

The men pack their gear without a word. In minutes the room is tidy but for the white suit hanging on a nail and the six identical packs lined up beside the door. The men step outside to piss, return and put in earplugs, blow out their candles and climb into bed. Their snoring soon fills the room.

While he waits for a second steak to cook, the culler tries to read. He watches his icy breath send shadows down the page. He can't concentrate. Scientists. Bullshit.

The door nicks open. It's Neil, late coming back from outside. He unrolls his sleeping bag on the boards. It occurs to the culler that there are only six bunks, and one of them is his.

Short straw? he says.

Something like that.

Go cut yourself some bracken. Better than those bunks. There's plenty up behind the hut.

Thanks, Neil says. But I'll be fine. You ever hear of method acting?

The culler looks at him. Neil shrugs, and climbs into his bag. He reads a notebook by firelight. His lips move, repeating phrases over and over in a whisper. Above the snapping fire and the river's distant drone it sounds like gibberish. *One's mall sleep foreman. One gaunt sleep firm and kind.*

After a few minutes Neil looks up. Have a listen to this garbage, he murmurs. *This is an historic moment, to be remembered as the triumph of a great nation's industry and vision.*

Who said that? the culler asks.

Me. Well, I'm supposed to say it.

What's it all about?

Neil thinks. Imagine you were the first person to climb a mountain. Everest, say, and you had to make a speech for the cameras on top. That's what it's about.

How'd you get a film camera on top of Mount Everest?

Well, Neil says, that's a damn good question.

The culler takes his pan from the coals and slides the steak onto his plate. So, are you a scientist, or a mountaineer, or what?

Neil doesn't reply. There's a look on his face the culler recognises from the war: when a person's brimming over with what they know. Then the young man's gaze strays to the sleepers in the adjacent bunks, and he shakes his head.

Tell me, he says, how long you spend out here? On your own?

The culler shrugs. Long as I can.

You're damn far from the world. How do you stay sane?

The culler slices the steak in two and holds out the plate. He keeps his gaze lowered when Neil grins and takes the piece. There are times he's had a deer in his sights and not squeezed the trigger, because he gets a sense that the animal is important. He's done the same with men. He can't decide if that makes him sane, or the opposite.

You weren't regular army, were you? Neil asks. Sniper?

The culler nods. He's used to the question from

wet-mouthed drunks, turned on by talk of headshots. Neil's curiosity seems different.

You worked by yourself? Same as out here?

Yeah. Why?

Just wondering. What was it like coming back?

Like coming back from outer space.

He'd come off the ship at Lyttleton, and followed the others into the pubs. He hadn't known where else to put himself. He wore the uniform everywhere, even to his father's funeral. Around the grave's raw edge the civilian crowd seemed ragged and disrespectful. At the wake his brother said to him, You need to move on, and he thought his brother was already speaking of their father. He'd meant the army. After the homecoming parades, the failed reinventions and third chances, the streets were still full of maimed drunks. The uniform earned no respect. He had a VC for bravery and he was afraid to sit in a parlour with his trigger finger crooked through the handle of a china teacup.

Too hard? Neil asks.

Hard enough.

Neil runs a hand along his jaw. It must be lonely out here, though. I think I'd miss people.

The culler laughs at that, a short bark. I miss people, he says. In a good way. This far from the world, you can forget what bastards they are. ·

People are bastards?

Trust me.

Neil shifts in his sleeping bag. What do you think of this, then? he says, riffling through his notebook with a chuckle. *For one priceless moment in the whole history of mankind, all people on this earth are truly one.*

Truly one? the culler says. Yeah. Truly mean.

C'mon. Neil sits up, grinning. You don't think that.

You think people are kind? You who's sleeping on the floor? Can't have any bacon?

Sure I do, Neil says. You who's telling me how to make a bed. Giving me venison.

Horseshit, the culler growls. That's not kindness. Any fool can do that. But he can't help himself: he likes the kid. His cheeks have mutinied into a grin.

There, Neil says. You see?

After a moment the culler settles back against the hearth. He jabs at the fading coals with a stick. The moon's visible through the window now, sitting above the black swell of the ridge beyond.

All those questions, the culler says. You're going away, aren't you?

Yeah.

More than a fortnight's field testing.

Same as you. Rest of my life.

Helluva trip. Where?

Ah shit, Neil says softly. I guess I can tell you.

The culler wakes before sunrise. He swings his legs over the edge of the bunk. The men are gone. There's ice on the window from their frozen breath. On the bench they've left him a pile of silver food tubes and a block of chocolate.

He pulls on his clothes, socks last. Where the wet wool hits his skin, tiny curls of steam rise and drift into the gloom. He carries his pack to the door.

He thinks of the men taking the white suit and the flag up the valley. Neil is wearing the suit as he walks, sealed from the world, with only the sound of his own breathing for company. He'll climb, slow and dreamlike, through cloud and ferns and the splintered beech brought low by last week's snow, till he's just a dot among the bluffs and peaks. He'll vanish into the moonscape, as far from civilisation as can be.

The culler slings his pack onto his back, shoulders his rifle and opens the door. The dawn valley gives him an icy lungful of pleasure. Mist fills the riverbed, while up above sunlight carves the shadowed lip of one ridge from the next.

He sees Neil planting the flag as the camera rolls, his face lost behind the mirrored visor. Neil will spend the rest of his life pretending. People will think he's changed forever. But he'll still be capable of kindness.

The culler launches himself from the top step of the hut into the world. He hears Neil's voice in his head. *That's one's mall sleep foreman. One gaunt sleep firm and kind.*

# ACKNOWLEDGEMENTS

To my family Geoff and Hikatea, Ben and Tim, thank you for the years of encouragement, stimulus and challenge, and the sense that stories are worth telling.

To Beth Ladwig, a thousand thanks for your critical insight, support and generosity, each of which made this book possible.

Thanks to my Stewart Street family—Stephen Mushin, Piers Gooding, Meg Hale, Robin Tregenza, Dom Kirchner and Imogen Hamel-Green—for enduring my long bush absences, and for all the coffees, dinners and discussions about characters like they were real people.

To everyone at Text, and particularly David Winter, thanks for your consummate skill in shaping raw material into polished work. The jokes in the margins were frequently better than the ones in the text.

A number of people provided invaluable critiques of early drafts. Thanks to Tim Low, Beth Ladwig, Hikatea Bull, Geoff Low, Stephen Mushin, Annie Zaidi, Jennifer Mills, Melissa Cranenburgh, Sam Gates-Scovell, and all the Monday night regulars. I owe a particular debt to Tom Doig for structural feedback that was on the money every time, and for *Moron to Moron*, the Mongolian inspiration behind the title story. That one's for you!

Thanks also to Lesley Alway and Asialink for the encouragement and trust in allowing me to juggle working and writing; the National Young Writers' Festival and This Is Not Art for the idea that it's okay to simply make shit up; *Griffith Review*, *Overland* and the *Big Issue* for getting behind early versions of three stories; Kerry Reid and Craig Gaston for being superb bush-neighbours and keeping me sane up there in the hills; and Marion M. Campbell for years of guidance at the University of Melbourne. I'm grateful to you all.